Search

Zombie Castle 4

Search

Chris Harris

PRESS

PRESS

First published by DHP Publishing in 2020
Published by Vulpine Press in the United Kingdom in 2025

Cover by Vulpine Press
ISBN: 978-1-83919-614-0

www.vulpine-press.com

CHAPTER ONE

The celebrations continued for a long time.

Never wavering from our goal, we'd travelled across hundreds of miles of zombie-infested wastelands, adding to our strength as individuals and other groups of survivors were found; our goal becoming the common goal as the concept of our destination was realised by all.

The brutal Darwinian nature of the world that was now the norm meant that the ones who had survived had found that something within them that they probably wouldn't have discovered in normal society. Something that made them endure when millions around them had perished, most screaming in agony as another's teeth ripped their living flesh from their bodies, before they themselves rose again to join the undead masses.

These people had not frozen in terror when faced with sights that their worst nightmare couldn't conjure up. They had done what they needed to do to live; to survive.

Most of them didn't know this themselves, just counting themselves lucky to have escaped and found somewhere safe to shelter. But they had it. That special thing that set them apart from others when the chips were down, and action needed to be taken.

The group was made up of a broad cross-section of society. From a vicar to a carpenter, a soldier to a retired childless housewife, everyone had contributed to the group's success. People from all walks of life, whose lives were so far apart from one another that they wouldn't normally even have mixed in the same circles or indeed have thought they could be friends; and we celebrated together as one.

Families had been torn apart. We knew with heart-breaking certainty that all our blood relatives had probably either succumbed to the virus and turned or had died in the ensuing chaos and panic.

Those gathered around us were our new family now.

Maud once again brought order to the group.

Raising her fingers to her mouth, she emitted a loud shrill whistle that caused all of us who were still laughing, hugging and dancing about to stop immediately and look in her direction.

"I'm sorry to ruin everybody's fun, but can we continue the celebrations later when we've made sure this place is safe? I can't let the children out of my sight until I know the whole place is clear."

Instantly brought down to earth by the matriarch of the group, most of us looked embarrassed as once again she had got the situation spot on. We did not know what lay behind any of the doors of the castle. And there were a lot of doors!

The group naturally gathered together and stood silently for a while, most looking around again at the castle, as I was, in a new light.

Was it safe? It looked it, but for us to truly know, we would have to carefully check every room and nook and cranny of the huge structure to be certain. That was going to be a monumental task that would need a great deal of coordination and organising so we could be sure that nothing was missed.

I turned to our experts in these matters. Sergeant Dave Eddy and Sergeant Simon Wood. "What do you think, guys?" Dave turned to Simon.

"Woody, if you block the gates, I'll start getting a squad together. I think it'll be best not to split up because things might get missed that way. If we leave ten on guard duty, do you think that will work?"

"Yeah, I reckon ten'll be enough," Simon replied. "If we're confident no more can get in and we form the usual square, no harm should come to them. And all they'd need to do is contact us on the radio or sound a horn and we'll not be far away." Simon turned to me.

"Tom, let's have a look at these gateways and work out the best way to block them up."

I nodded and together we walked over to the barbican. On the way a thought came into my head.

"I don't know why we haven't had this conversation before. We've got two Simons in our group and two Daves. It might avoid confusion if we call you something else. I know Simon's mates have been calling him Shitty after what happened to him when they first met some zombies, but I don't think the wife will be too happy if I keep calling him that in front of the children. How about we call you Woody?" Simon laughed.

"I vote for calling him Shitty. But I see your point. I suppose I can settle for Woody. Mind you, if I'd heard any of my men called me Woody before this happened, I'd have ripped them another arsehole. Only my mates and fellow sergeants could call me

3

it. We used to call Dave 'Eddy' because sometimes times there'd be a few Daves about, and it sort of made sense then. Once we get settled and safe here and to avoid any confusion, I don't think he'll mind either if we call him by his nick name."

Of the three gates that led into Warwick Castle, one was already barred with a heavy iron gate. It was as secure as it needed be for the time being, so we moved on. The barbican entrance didn't have any gates, but it still had the portcullis protruding from the ceiling.

Looking up, I remembered from my past visits to the castle witnessing it being lowered and raised as one of the attractions they performed. I didn't know where the mechanism was, and we didn't want to start opening doors to try to find it without more backup. Finding the winch room and closing the portcullis would be a matter of priority after we had searched the castle properly, but for now we decided that blocking it with a vehicle would suffice. The final gate, the one we'd driven through, was just an open arch built into the curtain wall and could easily be barred by positioning one of the vehicles across it.

Five minutes later, my Volvo was wedged at an angle into the barbican entrance. The extra sheeting and mesh we had surrounded the vehicle with made it wider and I just had to position it at an angle to block the way completely. I climbed out through the roof and scrambled down the bonnet of the car, had a quick look at my handy work to satisfy myself that the entrance was now completely blocked, and then I re-joined the others. The van was long enough to be parked across the other gate and block that too.

Dave in the meantime had organised who was doing what.

Maud and the children were asked to stay in the trailer that formed one side of the triangle of vehicles we'd created using the tractor, the Land Rover and the bus. Ten were chosen to remain and help to guard them and to keep the castle courtyard secured. For all we knew, zombies could appear out of any of the myriad of doors that opened onto it while we were searching other areas.

They were told not to take any risks and to get our attention if they thought they couldn't deal with a threat, and to wait for the main force to arrive. After all, they'd only be a few minutes away at most.

Jim was satisfied that he could leave the two we'd rescued from the retail park in the care of Maud and the others in the trailer. They were gaining strength with every hour that passed and had been able to tell us their story. It didn't take long to tell.

They'd all been on the early shift, restocking the shop before it opened. Unaware that anything was amiss, a few of them had opened the front door of the shop and stepped out for a cigarette break when a lone person staggered towards them from across the car park.

They were busy laughing at his antics as he approached, thinking he was a lost drunk still trying to find his way home after having way more than one too many. But as the man got nearer, they noticed the wounds on his face and the blood that was splashed over most of his clothes. Their mirth changed to concern as his UDIs (Unidentified Drinking Injuries) did seem serious.

A few called out to him, asking if he was okay but got no response. It was when he tripped up the kerb and fell flat on his face in front of them all that they went to his aid, with the now inevitable consequences. Thirty minutes later the three survivors found themselves trapped on top of some racking in the shop, surrounded by their former work colleagues. Unable to escape, what had kept them alive for so long was that the high racking they found themselves on contained some overstock for the shop. Amongst the boxes, they found a small quantity of energy drinks and protein bars which they had eked out for as long as they could. By the time we found them though, their supplies had long been consumed and they'd resigned themselves to a long, slow, lingering death by dehydration and starvation. Unaware even that their colleague who had been on the racking with them had died until we told them the sad news, they were unsure what emotion they felt more. Happiness to have been rescued and have a chance to live or sadness that their work colleagues and most likely their families had all gone.

Survivors' guilt was probably the best way to describe it. It was an emotion I didn't think any of us had had time to dwell upon much yet. In quiet times I found my mind wandering and the enormity of what had happened loomed large in my thoughts, as it probably did with all of us. But we had been continually busy and on the go so much that even the day of rest we'd had at the farm after the failed attempt to rescue Louise's parents was filled with many little jobs that kept our busy minds from wandering too far.

They weren't strong enough yet to do anything but lie down and take small, controlled sips of water and bites from energy bars. Jim assured us that they'd be back on their feet in no time if we continued what we were doing and didn't rush them or allow them to try to speed their own recovery along.

Those chosen to clear the castle gathered around Dave and Simon.

Simon began the briefing.

"Right then, ladies and gents. We have a massive task ahead of us." He waved his arms at the buildings surrounding us. "This place is freaking massive and until we've checked every single nook, cranny and cupboard, we'll not know if it's safe. I don't think we should split up but instead, we should work together to clear each area. I imagine that once we get a workable system sorted out, we should be able to check more than one room at a time, if we maintain communication and stay within easy reach of each other."

Then he looked at us all.

"Who's been here before and has an idea of the layout?" Chet, Becky and I raised our hands.

"Great. Can you all give us a rundown of what you remember about the place, please? It'll help us build up an idea of what we might expect."

I stepped forward and was about to speak when Becky put her hand on my shoulder and stopped me.

"Tom, what do you think you're doing, dear?" she asked softly with a smile on her face.

"I'm…er…going to tell them about the layout of the place. We were here last summer, if you remember," I replied, a little confused.

She laughed. "Right then. The person who forgets how old he is and what he ate for breakfast is going to give a guided tour from memory, when we last came here *two* years ago. Tom, do you want to leave it to someone who was actually paying attention when we did the guided tour and not just looking at the swords and guns?"

Again, I looked confused. "Did we have a tour?" My memory then returned, and I continued with a satisfied look spreading across my face. "Oh, yes we did, didn't we?"

"Exactly my point," she answered, before turning to Simon. "Shall I begin, Simon?"

Chuckling along with everyone else, he smiled and indicated for her to continue.

Becky then gave everyone a detailed description of the interior of the castle, describing each room the public was allowed in and pointing to their rough location in the structure.

I had to admit to myself her memory was impressive as she described each room and the different areas of the castle, from the state rooms to the restaurant, to what was in each of the towers that rose above the high curtain wall that surrounded the whole place. Her vivid descriptions even jogged my memory on rooms I'd forgotten about.

Once she'd finished, we all stood in silence as we looked around and tried to visualise and commit to memory all the information we'd just been given.

CHAPTER TWO

Room by room, we cleared the castle. Listening carefully at closed doors before opening them, we worked our way through the vast structure, slowly at first, but speeding up as our experience grew. Windows overlooking the courtyard gave us a clear view of the others waiting in the vehicles, so we didn't feel the need to check up on them or inform them of our progress as they could see us too and waved back when we got their attention.

The cellars proved to be the most daunting part. Pitch black due to no natural light entering them, we had to check each of the multitude of rooms by torchlight. Most of the rooms were used as part of the attractions of the place and so there were a lot of realistic dummies dressed in a variety of outfits going back through history, from knights in suits of armour to smaller ones portraying the children who used to work in the castle.

If it hadn't been so tense and scary it could have been funny, as many times we were shocked by seemingly lifelike characters 'jumping out' at us when suddenly lit by a passing beam of a torch. Geoff, on one occasion and much to our amusement afterwards when we eventually emerged into the sunlight, smashed the head off a mannequin that gave him a shock as he rounded a corner, and he didn't stop hitting it until his mace had turned the dressed-up dummy into a splintered pile of plastic and clothes as he vented his fear and shock on the inanimate object.

I called for a break when we had cleared the main building. We still had the towers and other rooms in the walls to clear. I didn't know about everyone else but the last few hours of tense searching, expecting to be attacked by a horde of flesh eaters at any moment, had taken it out of me.

Feeling secure enough, we sat on the open, grassed area by the vehicles. All the buildings we still had to check were a good distance away over the expansive inner court, so we would have plenty of warning if any zombies appeared. Opening the back of the trailer, we let the children and the dogs out so they could run around and expend some energy for a while. Of course, we needlessly warned them not to stray too far and to stay away from any of the buildings we had yet to search. With a chorus of agreement, they started to throw some tennis balls I had grabbed from the sports shop for this very purpose for the dogs to chase.

Horace, after a few minutes of what he obviously decided was unnecessary effort, came to join the adults sitting on the grass because he'd spotted Maud handing out mugs of hot drinks and snacks which he decided we needed to share with him. Once he'd received what he considered his rightful allocation, he lay content in the sun, his tail wagging lazily as he watched the children and Princess still happily playing.

"Well, what do you think of what we've seen so far, guys?" I asked with a smile as I sipped on my mug of tea.

Marc spoke. I hadn't had many opportunities to talk to him yet, but he seemed a really nice bloke. He was a distant acquaintance of the knights, but like Alex, not as close as the rest who had lived together for years. We'd heard his heart-breaking story of how he came to join them and so his quietness was understandable. But he was also often overshadowed by the larger than life personalities of Ian and the rest of the tight knit group of friends who were continually joking and trying to outdo each other on who seemed to be either the funniest or stupidest of the gang; that was, until they were brought back into line by the everpresent Maud. He didn't seem to mind not taking the limelight and had fought as hard and as well as the rest of them when needed.

"This place is better than I could ever have hoped for. It's bloody perfect! For God's sake, it's a fully functional working castle. What more could we want? It's big enough to house us all ten times over, easily. The walls, once we block the gates up properly…well, they were built to withstand a siege after all, they'll keep us safe for as long as we need them to."

Everyone agreed with his summary and we spent the rest of the time while we finished the mugs of tea and snacks chatting about the castle; particularly, from what we'd seen so far, how we could make the castle liveable and more secure.

Becky had found a guidebook when we were searching which had a detailed map of the castle, including all the rooms it contained. She marked on it all the rooms we'd searched so far. If anything, it showed us how much ground we had still to cover and reminded us we'd better get on with it. Despite their protests, we insisted the children return to the safety of the trailer until we knew it was completely clear of any zombies.

Working clockwise around the walls, we continued the task. Investigating the mound, we discovered much to our chagrin a missed archway in the walls at the top of the mound: the original part of the castle dating from the Norman conquest of England in the eleventh century. It had been hidden behind the ornamental bushes that had been planted on the steep conical hill so we couldn't see it from the inner court below.

Becky, Chet and I, had all been to the castle before and we apologised for forgetting about the potentially dangerous error in our memory.

It did have a steel, hinged gate which in the past would have been used to close it but it was rusted up and even though we all tried, none of us could free it from its years of neglect.

"Don't worry about it," said Woody as he walked through the archway and from our elevated position, surveyed the grounds that stretched out before us. "No harm done. This little hill has got such steep sides, I imagine it'd be hard for those bastards to climb it anyway. With the stuff we have with us, we should be able to block this up easily." He turned and looked at the archway and then looked at Shawn. "Can you have a go at it now, mate?"

Shawn replied as he looked at the six-foot-wide gap. "No problems. If I drag the genny up here along with some timber and some sheeting, I can block it up in no time. Who can I have to help me? It'll take two of us to get the genny up here."

Becky interrupted. "Why don't you leave the generator at the bottom of the hill and use an extension cable if it's that heavy?"

Shawn looked at her with a 'duh! Why didn't I think of that' expression on his face.

Woody responded, laughing, "And that, gents, is why men are doomed without the fairer sex." He pointed at Jon and Jamie. "Great idea, Becky. Jon if you can help him and if you, Jamie, could guard them, just in case, we'll carry on checking the rest of this place out."

Shawn looked a bit apprehensive as he inspected the stonework of the doorway.

"What's up?" I asked as I began to walk away with the rest of the group.

"Oh, nothing really. It's just, I've worked on listed buildings before and you can't even stick a screw in the walls sometimes under pain of a proper bollocking from the Historic England people. I know we need to, but it seems sacrilege to use a hammer drill on these walls. That's all." He laughed and held his hands up. "I know, I know, I'll get over it." He turned to Jon and Jamie. "Let's get on with it. Jamie, if you stay up here and guard the gap, Jon and I will go and get the stuff we need from the trailer."

Slowly checking every room, cupboard and nook and cranny, we continued working around the building, finding nothing until we reached the large impressive fortified main gate of the castle, known as the barbican. We could hear power tools operating as Shawn and Jon worked on blocking up the hole in the walls. The loud screeching hammering of his drill worried me. So far, we'd tried to be as quiet as possible and the noise he was making, even though it was unavoidable, would certainly be loud enough to be heard beyond the castle grounds, potentially attracting unwelcome visitors. We hadn't had chance to survey any of the perimeter fences surrounding the castle yet. We hoped they were as secure and intact as the emptiness of the place indicated, but until we'd physically checked them, we couldn't be sure.

Dave Eddy had his ear to the door with a sign on it saying, 'security office', when he held his hand up to get our attention, before turning and whispering, "I think there's someone in here."

We all raised our weapons and stared at the door as he slowly backed away from it, indicating with a wave of his arm for us to walk further away, back down the corridor we'd just cleared.

"It makes sense," began Eddy, "if there was anyone here overnight, it would be the security guys. And apart from any foot patrols they might need to do, I imagine they would mainly just sit in an office, watching the feed from security cameras." He paused and looked at the knights. "Okay, guys, usual drill. I'll check the door to see if it's unlocked. If it is, I'll open it and step back for you to enter, shields first. If it's locked…" He looked at the hulking shape of Ian as he stood looking like a man mountain in his armour. "I'm sure your size fourteen feet can open the door just like they have with all the other locked ones we've found. The rest of you watch our backs in case the noise we're bound to make brings any more of them out of the woodwork." He paused and looked at us all. "Ready?"

When we all nodded in agreement, he waited for the knights to get into formation behind him, before reaching out and pushing down on the door handle. He pushed it down and the door clicked loudly in the silence as the latch released. A groaning noise we'd got to know well sounded through the still closed door and something crashed into it from the inside, making it rattle on its frame, and we all jumped back slightly.

Eddy looked at Ian, nodded and stepped back to give him some space. More bangs came from the door.

"Sounds like there's more than one in there," Ian said as he steadied himself before uttering, "Ready, boys!" He took a pace forward and raising his armour-clad leg, smashed it into the door. The door burst open. The groans were replaced by crashing noises as whatever was behind it was knocked over by the power of his kick.

With a shout of, "Come on, lads," Ian regained his balance and with his axe held ready, raised his shield and stepped through the doorway, closely followed by the rest of the knights.

We couldn't see what was happening but the grunts, shouts and now familiar sounds of blades striking soft flesh and bone brought up a vivid picture of the carnage the knights could rain on the undead.

After a final flurry of noise, in the silence that followed, a call of, "All clear" came through the doorway. We trooped in. The remains of four bodies, all either with no head or a severely damaged one, lay at various angles on the floor. Blood and pieces of skull and brain stuck to or slowly slid down the bank of monitors that filled one half of the room. Looking around the room, we could see another a pile of bones and clothes in a corner and it told an all too familiar story of someone's last moments filled with terror and pain as their former colleagues ate them alive.

The room was large and clearly used as the security office for the castle. There were desks for people to work at, some comfortable chairs and tables at one end, with a small kitchen area for taking breaks, and one wall was filled with banks of screens and control panels for the clearly high-tech security system the castle possessed.

Looking at the blank, lifeless screens, we all came to the same conclusion: if we could get it up and running again, it would be a great boost to our overall security and ability to spot any threats approaching the walls.

Geoff was wiping the blood off his mace with some cloths he'd found in the kitchen and he looked up and said, "We need Shawn to have a look at all this. He might understate what he does, but he's a bloody good electrician and I know he installed big systems like this when he worked on the oil rigs. If we get him some power here, I've no doubt he can get it going again."

I saw Becky looking pensive. I walked up to her, put my arm around her and kissed her forehead. "You okay, darling?" I asked.

"Yes, you've got me thinking," she said as she pulled the map of the castle from her pocket. "Do you remember the mill that's attached to the castle? Didn't one of the old owners convert it to generate electricity back in the old days?" She pointed on the map to those of us close by to the mill that was attached to the castle, but near to the river. "I think it still works. Well, I remember it was doing something when we went."

I remembered it now. When it was installed in the late 1800s it was a marvel of the modern age and I think it provided enough power to light the castle.

I kissed her again. "Bloody brilliant, darling. Well remembered."

I looked at Woody and Eddy. Woody replied with a look of mock disgust on his smiling face. "Thanks, Becky! More work for us all." He looked out of the window at the view of the castle grounds and then at his watch. The sun was getting lower in the sky. There were still a few hours of daylight left, but it was still getting late in the day. "Let's get the rest of this place cleared and then everyone unloaded and inside first. If we have time then, we can check further afield, but I think most of us are about done in. The priority is getting us a safe place for the night. Tomorrow we can start making plans for the whole place. But yes, I agree if we can get the CCTV up and running, that would be brilliant. Becky, can I have a look at the map, please?" She handed it over and he studied it for a few moments.

"Right, it looks like we've got most of the place ticked off as checked, so let's carry on and get the job done." He looked at the corpses on the floor and gave the nearest one a kick. "First job after that will be to get those out of here. They're smelling bad enough already, if we leave them till tomorrow, they'll stink the whole place out."

We quickly but thoroughly scoured the remaining rooms and finding them deserted, we returned to the inner courtyard and our vehicles.

Maud, looking down at us from the side of the trailer, was holding a crying Sarah. "Is it safe?"

Becky looked up at her. "Yes, Maud. We can get you down and find somewhere more comfortable now."

She looked relieved as she answered. "That's good news. It's too hot out here for poor Sarah. She'll be much happier if we can get her into somewhere cooler."

"I think you'll like our new home, Maud. Can you think what you'll need to get unloaded first and we'll get you and the kids settled in."

Maud looked at the faces of our children who were peering over the sides of the trailer. "Oh, don't worry. I think the youngsters have enough energy to help carry a few boxes. Haven't you, children?"

All the children announced their agreement cheerfully.

Showing once again how important Maud was to our little group, not only had she kept the children occupied while we were searching the castle, but she'd also cared for the two we'd rescued from the outdoor supplies warehouse. This had freed more of our group to guard them or to help make sure the place was clear of any danger.

Forty-four people and two dogs started moving into our new home. The four former occupiers were dumped unceremoniously into an industrial sized waste bin we found hidden behind some fencing for disposal in the morning.

CHAPTER THREE

We didn't unload everything we had from the vehicles, only taking what we needed to make us comfortable for the night. The castle had so many rooms we could use and so many doors to access the various parts, that until we decided who and what was going where, it seemed a waste of time to unload the large amount of supplies and equipment we had until got more organised.

Discussing if we needed to organise a guard rota, we decided that until we were more familiar with the castle and set a proper system in place, we could be putting ourselves at unnecessary risk. Parking the vehicles to protect the main door to the castle, we closed and bolted the huge wooden doors, sealing ourselves in for the night. The windows overlooking the inner courtyard gave us a clear view of its large expanse of grass, so Woody quickly sorted out a rota, stationing one of us to sit in the window of the state dining room keeping watch, just in case anybody or anything managed to breach the defences.

For safety, we also limited everyone to the main ground floor rooms of the castle and secured any doors that led into other areas. The Great Hall was the obvious place from the more than ten rooms we had to choose from for us to gather. It was an incredibly impressive, large room with huge windows overlooking the River Avon and its walls were lined with suits of armour and arrays of weapons. It perfectly portrayed the grandeur and wealth of the Earls of Warwick who had resided in the castle for the hundreds of years before it was turned into an attraction. It even had two full-sized knights mounted on their destriers guarding the room.

The high ceilings and thick stone walls provided a welcome relief from the heat of the day and while some began to sort through the supplies we'd brought inside, others dragged enough chairs, sofas and other furniture into the room from elsewhere for us all to sit on.

Released by Maud from their duties, the children ran about excitedly exploring the rooms, for once free of the ever-watchful eyes of their parents, who knew for the first time in many days that no danger could befall them.

While I sat in a comfortable chair, my legs stretched out in front of me, I could feel my body begin to relax. We'd made it against all the odds. We still had a massive amount of work ahead of us and that would probably never end if we wanted to survive the coming days, weeks, months and possibly years. But for now, we were safe in what was possibly the best place in the country to ride out the terror that had consumed the entire planet.

The knights seemed to be the most excited of us all to be in the room; they gawped in wonder at the array of weapons on the walls and suits of armour the room was filled with.

I watched, amused, at Simon trying to prise a sword out of the hand of a plate armour-clad figure. Calling over to him, I jokingly admonished him, "Oi, it's not a bloody jumble sale, you know."

By now, he'd managed to free the sword from its previous owner's grip, and he gave it a few practice swings before holding it with both hands and admiring it.

"Aw, come on, mate. These weapons are the real deal, not the reproduction ones we use. There's no way I could afford this beauty; it's got such great balance I could swing it for hours and not get tired." He ran a finger carefully across the edge of the weapon. "A few hours with a whetstone and I'll get this baby as sharp as when…" He turned to look at the small information sign that was next to the figure. He jolted with physical shock and then stared with reverence at the weapon, before quietly muttering as if in disbelief.

"Bloody hell, it's only Richard Neville's sword, the King Maker himself!"

He stood, looking unsure at what he should now do with the almost six-hundred-year-old personal weapon of one the most important persons in English history. The rest of his friends, hearing what he'd said, crowded round to look at the weapon.

Ian read the information sign. "It's his bleeding armour too!" And he tried to take the full-face helmet off the figure. He pulled too hard and it toppled over, crashing onto the hard-stone floor of the Great Hall with the sound of dozens of metal pans being dropped from a great height.

Sarah, who was sleeping in the wicker basket we'd turned into a cot for her, woke with a startled cry and began wailing in shock and outrage. The knights, looking very contrite, stood frozen in horror at what they'd done until Maud, who'd reached Sarah first and picked her up in an effort to console the screaming baby, turned to them.

The tone of her voice and the look on her face told them they were in deep trouble. "Ian. Why is it always you? You lumber about like a big oaf, not thinking of the consequences of what you're doing until it's too late. Do you know how long it had taken us to get her to sleep?"

She gently held Sarah out in front of her. "Well, you can try now."

She looked at the petrified expression on his face as he realised she wanted him to have Sarah. "Yes, you! Come here and get her back to sleep. It might make you think next time before you do something stupid."

His friends stepped back slightly, smiling with relief in knowing that, once again, Ian was taking the brunt of her anger. Ian slowly shuffled towards Maud, his eyes staring fearfully at the crying face peering out of the blankets she was wrapped in.

He tentatively held his arms out as Maud carefully placed Sarah into the grip of his huge hands. Ian immediately adopted the pose people who are unused to holding babies adopt; hunched over and acting like they're holding a priceless, very fragile antique vase. She immediately stopped crying and her small arms reached out to touch his face. He looked up in amazed triumph and tried to hand her back, but as soon as she left the comfort of his enveloping hold, she began wailing again.

Maud smiled at him. "Oh no, it's not that easy, big man. Keep walking around with her until she is truly asleep." As he pulled her close to him, she stopped crying once more. Staring at her, his terrified look softened and changed to one of amazement and joy at the baby, who was now smiling and giggling at him. Without another word, he turned and began walking around the room, jiggling her softly and making cooing noises.

Eventually he noticed the women were looking at him the way only a woman can when looking at a man holding a cute baby.

He couldn't help himself as he addressed the room but looked pointedly at Shawn standing next to Louise.

"Watch out, boys. Not only am I the most attractive man here, but I am also a baby whisperer. No woman in her right mind will be able to resist me now."

Once the laughter had settled down, Maud spotted the rest of the knights, who were beginning to look at and touch the weapons again and she raised her voice once more. "Can you stop it? It's a privilege for us to be here and I don't want this beautiful room ruined by your ham-fisted efforts to get some new toys. I'm sure once we have investigated every room fully, there'll be plenty more things lying around for you to take, so you can leave this place alone for now."

With a few grunts, the knights reluctantly agreed and stepped back from the weapon-filled walls, and the group settled down to begin collectively cooking a meal on the camping stoves we'd unloaded, and organising areas where we could all sleep. There were enough rooms to afford families and couples a degree of privacy each, which after being so long in close company with each other would be something we were all grateful for. We knew there were enough rooms in the rest of the buildings and even some apartments which they rented to those who wanted to experience living in a castle, so in the future there was a good chance that most would be able to have their own quarters. But for now, everyone was more than happy to share the large and beautiful 'show' rooms the castle had.

The two we had rescued from the warehouse, Faye and Dominic, were gaining strength and were able to join us. Once the parents amongst us had eventually got the reluctant children to sleep, we got together in the Great Hall in the gathering darkness. We collected candles in ornately gilded holders from various rooms and the adults sat in the room lit by their flickering flames.

We opened some beer and wine, and we discussed and planned what we needed to do the following day.

CHAPTER FOUR

I was rostered on the early morning lookout duty shift. Once Noah woke me up, I quietly made myself a mug of coffee and sat by one of the state dining room windows overlooking the inner courtyard. Waiting for the sun to start rising, occasionally sweeping the light from a powerful torch slowly around the area, I thought about the day ahead and what we had planned.

Firstly, before we allowed anyone to start roaming freely, we wanted to conduct another full check of all the buildings, just in case we'd missed anything first time around. Louise had suggested the night before that it would be a good idea to mark the door of every room we'd checked as clear. That way, if we came across a door without a mark on it, we would know we'd missed one. Daisy's bag provided us with a few sticks of chalk which would be great for the job.

Chris had suggested we block any entrance we didn't need to use with either bricks or blocks as a permanent fix. The vehicles we were using at the current time could only be a temporary solution and if bricks or blocks were laid correctly, they'd be just as strong as the rest of the ancient walls. We'd agreed that while others were doing the final sweep of the castle, he would measure up and work out what was required to do the job. There'd be a builders' merchant somewhere in Warwick where we would be able to find all he'd need; to that end, we were on the lookout for a telephone directory or yellow pages so we could locate the nearest one and save time driving around finding it.

My first task would be to find the winch room to try and close the portcullis on the barbican entrance. I remembered from our previous visit it seemed very sturdy. Once we'd closed it, we would be able to see if anything else was needed to strengthen or improve it for our purpose.

As the light strengthened in the growing dawn, people started to stir. Thankfully, the inner courtyard had remained clear so at least our initial defences had worked. I was sure by the end of the day they'd be even better.

To save us splitting into multiple groups, I asked Chris to join me and the few I'd enlisted to help me with the portcullis. It wouldn't take him long to estimate how many bricks or blocks he'd need to do the work, and it would mean we could stay together and we wouldn't need so many people to guard us; in turn, that would free up more to recheck the castle more quickly.

Once we'd had a few cups of tea and breakfast, we got ready to venture out.

***

"Shit!" was all I needed to say to get everyone alert as we approached the van that was blocking the largest 'gap' in the castle's walls.

The unmistakable groaning sound of zombies could be heard beyond it. Cautiously approaching the van, I looked through the mesh-covered passenger window. Beyond the other side of the van I could see zombies staggering past. Holding my fingers up to my lips to keep everyone quiet, I pointed to Shawn and indicated for him to get the others, who'd already begun their search of the castle. Nodding, he turned and ran to find them. I winced at the metallic noises his armour made as he moved.

In no time at all he'd returned and I waved for them to be quiet as they approached. Woody took a quick look through the van window and summed it up in one word, as I had.

"Shit!" He gave a rueful shrug as he looked at us all. "Time to get to work again, folks." He looked at Eddy. "How do you want to do this, mate?"

"Let's have a look from the walls and work out how many we're dealing with first. There doesn't seem to be masses of them out there, but they're getting in from somewhere."

Steps led up to the ramparts next to the arch, so trying to keep as quiet as possible, everyone walked up the ancient stone steps. Looking more like tourists, we all leant over the wall and looked down. Around forty zombies were milling around the grassed area below us and more were approaching, staggering along in single file from where I knew the perimeter fence to be.

Stating the obvious, I said. "There must be a hole in the fence up there somewhere. I suppose all the noise we made arriving yesterday and then using drills to make the frame to block up the gateway attracted them from the town."

Having seen enough, Eddy got our attention and we gathered around him. "Let's play this safe. If we get some of those silenced .22 rifles we have, we can get most of them from up here. Then Simon can do a sweep of the grounds in the Defender, getting any we miss." He turned and looked at Shane. "Shane, lad, can you go and get some of those .22s, please?"

He nodded and we watched him descend the staircase and run across the courtyard and emerge a few minutes later from the main building, walking slightly more awkwardly this time as he was encumbered with rifles slung over both shoulders. Woody and Eddy both helped him as he arrived out of breath back on the ramparts and took the guns from him.

"Thanks, mate," Woody told him and then held the guns out. "Let's use this as another training ex. Who hasn't used these before? Now's as good a time as any and it'll also be a good way of checking if they're sighted correctly."

I'd used .22s before as it was the first rifle I'd got from the farmhouse what seemed weeks before on the moors, but which was in reality only days ago. We'd got many more when we cleared the gun shop where we found Shane. But most of the training and experience everyone else had was with the military rifles we'd scavenged from Bickley barracks. These provided a higher rate of fire and heavier calibre bullets which, when firing from the sides of vehicles or when facing a pack of them on foot, had proved to be the most effective to use, along with the shotguns.

The .22s, we knew, would make an excellent short-to-medium-range sniper rifle and we had many thousands of the small, lightweight bullets for them and knew we could get many thousands more, because they were a popular, if not the most popular, rifle bullet available from gun shops across the UK.

After a few minutes getting the ones who said they wanted to practise with them into position, the rest of us lined the walls and leant against them. We peered down at the zombies below us, again looking more like the tourists who on a normal day would be lining the walls and admiring the views from the elevated position the walls offered, and not doing as we were getting ready to; watching the killing of yet more of the undead.

The pinging of the brass cartridges as they were ejected from the guns was louder than the muted popping of them firing. Woody, Eddy and Shane helped everyone, giving tips and advice as they familiarised themselves with the firearms. From the elevated firing position, the moving heads of the zombies provided a tantalising but small target, which initially most found hard to hit. Frustration was kept at bay as their instructors all explained that shooting at an angle down from height was a difficult skill to learn. The small bullets also made it difficult to mark the fall of shot. The zombies were staggering as they shambled along, so a hit from a bullet was difficult to distinguish as they only fell to the floor when the subsonic bullet entered their skulls and destroyed the brain.

But with encouragement from the watchers and help from the instructors, their accuracy improved and slowly the ones lying still on the ground began to outnumber the ones standing, their heads turning and their teeth gnashing together as they searched out their next victim until a bullet destroyed their brain.

Eventually, Woody called out for everyone to stop firing. All those in effective range had been re-killed and it was now clear in front of the gates.

"Okay, guys," he called out cheerfully. "Well done, everyone. That'll do for now. We still have to check out the inside of the castle one more time, so could four of you stay up here and continue getting any that keep appearing? The rest of us will carry on and do that."

The four volunteers began reloading magazines from open boxes of bullets and then rested their weapons on the ramparts, ready for use, as the rest of us checked our own weapon and listened to Woody's and Eddy's instructions about how they were going to conduct the sweep.

As initially intended, we would start by trying to lower the portcullis to seal the barbican entrance up completely and then we would check every room again, marking every door this time with chalk to avoid any room being missed. We were to follow the same plan as yesterday and stay together as one group. With the numbers we had, it enabled us to leapfrog each other and check more than one room at a time.

The four sharpshooters were reminded to keep checking the ramparts and the area around them, just in case any appeared unexpectedly from somewhere we'd missed on our previous search, potentially catching them unawares when their attention was fixed beyond the walls.

CHAPTER FIVE

On entering the cool, shaded, tunnel-like entrance of the barbican, we could see a few zombies had crossed the stone bridge that crossed the moat and were pushing against my car that I'd jammed into the narrow passageway yesterday, blocking it completely. They couldn't get near us, but it also meant we couldn't get to them easily.

I turned to Woody. "What are we going to do about that lot?" I asked quietly, so as not to attract their attention while waving my arms towards them. "I don't think we can see or get to them from the walls."

He stared at them and then looked at the rest of us with a calculating look on his face.

"We could climb onto your car and shoot them." I nodded and began to reach for my rifle. "But also, your car is right under the portcullis we want to lower, so why don't we kill the proverbial two birds with one stone? There aren't too many of them, so if you climb in and pull your car forward, the rest of us will go and deal with them. If you pull back and block the entrance again and then act as rear gunner if anything goes wrong, we should have them dealt with in no time at all."

His eyes glanced at everyone else who was crowding around listening to his low whispering voice. Not seeing any disagreement and nodding in reply to the general gripping of weapons and looks of determination he received as an answer, he continued.

"Okay then, guys and gals. Usual stuff. Let the knights lead the way and we'll provide cover and support. Any questions?"

Again no one spoke up so as I climbed into my Volvo, he led the rest back into the courtyard. Standing on the bonnet of my car, I leaned in and placed my rifle on the passenger seat before clambering in. Retrieving the keys from where I'd stashed them behind the sun visor, I glanced unconcernedly at the few zombies ineffectually pawing at the mesh that covered the rear window of the car and turned the ignition.

In the bright sunlight ahead, I could see the others looking in my direction, so with a thumbs-up to tell them to get ready, I put the car in drive and depressed the accelerator. The car was wedged in tightly, so I had to apply more power before, with a screech of protesting metal, I freed it and pulled forward.

I stopped to leave a gap large enough, and the knights led the group at a jog as they advanced into the fray once more. Pulling back to block the entrance again, I stood on my seat and grabbing my rifle, raised it ready.

The knights had linked shields and, as one, were slowly advancing through the barbican. If a film crew had been present, it could have been mistaken for the shooting of a scene from a historical film or even a flashback in time. The backdrop of the ancient barbican entrance and knights in full armour looked so realistic.

From my elevated position I could see axes and swords rising and falling as without missing a step, they ploughed through the undead. Standing, I once again thought how calm I felt, and by the way everyone was acting, they looked to be feeling it, too. Yes, they were facing up to and killing more former human beings, but we knew that in small numbers, if no one messed up, they were relatively easy to deal with, given the weapons we had.

Woody and Eddy both kept continually telling us about how complacency would kill you and they were correct. We only had one chance to get it right and the cost of failure would be someone in the group paying the ultimate price. I thought, though, that we all took it as a compliment that they needed to keep telling us, but as I stood watching my friends killing more of them, not at one point did I feel anxious. The few they were facing were nothing to what they had faced before and most likely would do again.

Now we were at our destination, we were in a much better position. We could more easily pick the fights we could win, and if not, we could retreat behind the walls and either deal with the threat or wait it out.

Woody shouting to me broke me from my wandering thoughts.

"All clear, pal. We'll hold the gate if you want to find the portcullis control thingy."

Smiling at his description, I grabbed the ladder attached to the front of the car and wrestled it into position so I could climb down the rear of it and then walked into the passageway. A small ancient looking wooden door set into the stonework of the passageway caught my eye. It had a modern lock set into its wide oak boards. Logically, it would be the place to house the entrance to the winding gear, because in the past it would have been close

33

enough to enable the guards at the gate to seal the castle quickly in times of trouble.

Finding the door locked when I tried it, I shouted for some help to open it. Geoff, his mace over his shoulder, turned from the group guarding the entrance and made his way over to me. He took one look at the door, told me to stand clear and aimed a powerful swing at the lock. The door rattled in its frame and splintered where he'd hit it, but the lock held.

He looked at me, shrugged, and holding his mace out for me to take, took a few paces back before running at it and smashing his mail clad shoulder against the stubborn door.

Not being able to help myself, I had to laugh as he bounced off it and ended up in a pile on the floor, emitting a string of curses as he tried to decide what hurt more, his pride or his shoulder. The rattling noise of his armour meeting the hard, stone floor attracted the attention of his friends, who all offered a few words of sympathy and support.

Okay, no they didn't, they all hooted with laughter and shouted sarcastic comments.

Ian lumbered up with a big grin on his face and held out a hand to help his struggling friend to his feet. "Care to let a real man have a go?" he said as he handed me his axe.

Weighted down with both a heavy mace and now a huge axe, I had to rest both on the ground quickly before I dropped them.

Ian theatrically studied the door, tutting at the damage Geoff had caused before pulling a knife from a sheath in his belt and inserting it in between the door and frame. He gave a small push, the lock clicked, and the door swung open. Keeping a straight face, he sheathed his knife and took his axe from me before looking at an open-mouthed Geoff and adopting an atrocious Chinese accent, said,

"As Sun Tzu say. Power of man not come from muscle, but from strength of brain." He then walked jauntily back down to the ones guarding the entrance.

Geoff looked at his receding back, shaking his head in disbelief.

"Come on, mate," I said, slapping him on his back. "Let's check the room's clear. It might not even be the right one after all."

Geoff, all business again, raised his mace and stepped towards the open door, stooping slightly as he poked his large frame into the small opening. "It's the one," he called back, his voice echoing slightly as he stepped inside. "And it's clear."

I followed him into the narrow stone passage that led to a small circular room illuminated by the light streaming through the arrow slits set into its walls. The room contained the winding gear for the portcullis. Surprised at the simplicity of it, I studied it for a short while. A rope that stretched to the ceiling and disappeared through a small hole was attached around a small drum with a handle that was bolted to the floor. Another rope, which I assumed was the other end of the one that went through the ceiling, hung down and had a large lead weight attached to it that hung above a small hole in the floor. I surmised the lead weight was the counterbalance, designed to take the weight of the portcullis and make it easier to operate. It was an incredibly simple design, but cleverly conceived, nonetheless.

I remarked to Geoff, who was standing next to me, also inspecting the winding gear, "Look at it, it's genius. Those old boys certainly knew what they were doing. Come on then, let's try it out."

I took hold of the handle and turned it. The rope tightened, but after half a turn it stopped moving. Putting more weight on it, I leant on the handle more, but it still didn't move.

"Hang on a bit," Geoff said and stepped forward, putting his mace down. "I think that length of timber is stopping it. Wind back on the rope a bit, mate and I'll try and move it."

Seeing what he was indicating, I nodded and reversed the direction I was winding. The rope tightened again, and Geoff reached for the length of timber. After fiddling with it for a few seconds, he noticed a pin that was holding it in place, removed it and the timber moved easily. Immediately, I felt weight on the winding mechanism and held the handle tightly.

"Geoff, mate," I said, "go and tell 'em outside that the portcullis should be closing now and to get the right side of it."

I waited, holding the handle, until Geoff walked down the short passage and called out of the door for those outside to take care.

Walking back down the passage, he gave me the thumbs-up and I turned the handle. A low scraping sound and slight knocking coming through the handle told me something was happening. The counterweight lifted from its position and slowly rose to the ceiling, until with a slight thud, the weight went off the mechanism.

Eddy poked his head through the door and called, "Good work, lads, it's down."

Smiling with satisfaction, I walked down the passageway and joined the others in the tunnel that led through the barbican. The portcullis was down. Approaching it, I grabbed one of the thick timber lattices that made up the huge wooden construction and shook it. The portcullis would easily, as it was originally designed to do, provide a second line of defence for the castle's main gate.

If any attacker had broken through the raised drawbridge, which sadly was no longer there, they would have to face the spears and arrows of the defenders as they stood behind it.

Chris came and stood next to me and he, too, grabbed the woodwork and gave it a tug. "Solid as a rock, mate," he said with a smile, admiring the hundreds-of-years-old structure. "Not much to do here. Maybe just covering it with boards to stop anything seeing in would help." He pointed across the bridge which spanned the deep moat. "Maybe if we build a gate or something at the end of the bridge it'll stop anything getting close to it, but it'll do for now."

"Good idea," I said slapping him on the back. "Keep those ideas coming. Just keep your notepad out, writing down what we need. When we get the perimeter outside secure, then fortifying this place will be top of the to-do list, I'm sure."

Saying that reminded me we still had a job to do, so I went to join the others.

Working together, it took over an hour to carefully recheck everywhere we'd been the day before, this time, though, marking every door as clear with the chalk we had with us. Finding a few more rooms and passages we'd missed the day before proved that the precaution of rechecking had been a worthwhile venture. Thankfully, and to our relief, they contained no surprises, but it reminded us once again how vast Warwick Castle actually was.

CHAPTER SIX

Returning to the others who were waiting in the Great Hall of the castle for the final all-clear to be given, we found they hadn't been idle in our absence. More furniture had been moved, creating a seating area surrounding the huge fireplace large enough to accommodate us all. Another room was planned to be the cooking area and the few camping stoves we'd unloaded along with food had already been positioned and the furniture the room contained had been moved elsewhere.

As we shrugged out of our tactical vests and the knights removed some of their armour to make themselves more comfortable, Maud, still bustling around, getting others to move items around to exactly where she wanted them, had to be ordered to sit down, rest, and let others do something. Once Becky had removed her own tactical vest, she joined in, leaning her gun up against the wall, next to everyone else's. Becky told Maud she didn't need to keep proving her worth as she was already 'the boss' and if she worked herself to the point of exhaustion, then who else would keep the 'stupid' men in line.

Maud, bless her, got emotional as we guided her to the comfiest armchair and placed a mug of tea in her hands.

Thanking us for our kindness, saying in all her long and tortuous years of marriage to her husband, she'd had more respect and love in the last few days than she'd received in her life before.

Ian, who once again couldn't stop himself, hugged her and jokingly asked if he could call her granny or aunty. All he got for his failed effort at humour was a stern command from Maud, trying to hide her amusement. She promised that he was now on dishwashing duty until she decided otherwise and told him to take the tray of mugs of tea up to the ones on the walls who were still sniping at the zombies coming through the hole in the fence. Beaten once more, he shambled off, muttering comically to himself.

We didn't spend our tea break idly. Now we were sure the castle was clear, we had to plan the mission to secure the grounds. Watching from the walls, we could see the rough location the zombies were getting in from, as they stubbornly kept appearing from the same direction. The trailer Simon towed behind his Land Rover still contained a large quantity of materials we'd collected from the farmers' supply shop near Bristol, so we were confident that with what we had, we should be able to secure whatever breach we found.

Adopting our proven 'strength in numbers' ideology, we decided to take both the tractor and Woody's Land Rover with his trailer carrying the supplies. The machine guns mounted on both the car and trailer behind the tractor would provide all the heavy fire support we would need, along with the shooters, to keep us all safe. Once we'd found and repaired the hole they were using for access, we'd carry on to conduct a thorough search of the rest of the perimeter and secure, strengthen or repair any other weak points we found.

It was another huge task, as the perimeter fence had to be very long, due to the size of the grounds. Eddy and Woody, eager to complete the task, encouraged us all to finish the bowls of food that had been handed around and finish our mugs of tea so we could get on with it.

We'd found more radios in the camping shop, so we inserted batteries into them, then tested them and set them to the same channel. The people who'd been chosen to stay and guard the castle were allocated positions and then given a radio so they could easily contact us all. Some were told to stay with Maud and the children while others were positioned around the walls, where they could spot danger approaching from all directions.

The rest of us would be either in the Land Rover with Woody or in the trailer towed by Shawn. Once the van was moved from where it blocked the open archway, we'd all drive into the grounds and get to work.

The sharpshooters on the walls had continued sniping at the steady flow of zombies as they appeared and the ground below their position was becoming littered with their handiwork. They were all pleased with how their accuracy had improved. As they descended the stairs from the ramparts and handed the .22 rifles to those chosen to replace them on the walls, they happily went to their next assigned position, eager to help with the next task.

Stopping the small convoy just outside the gate, we waited for the van to pull back into position before driving across the well-tended lawns, following the trail of zombies; all lying still with a small red hole in their foreheads.

A zombie pushing through what was now a reasonably well-worn trail through some undergrowth pinpointed the location for us. Stopping, Noah leaned over the side of the trailer and drove his spear through the top of the zombie's head. More could be heard pushing through the bushes when the engines were turned off. Woody stood up on his seat.

"Right then, knights, time to earn your pay again. If the rest of us cover you, can you go and see what's up with the fence, please?"

I was in the trailer, so I helped open the rear door and lower the ramp, allowing the knights to exit. With shields raised, they walked one-by-one down the ramp and formed a shield wall facing the dense bushes, studying them intently.

"Right then," called Jamie, assuming command. "For once, my compact muscular build is an advantage over the rest of you blundering oafs. I'll lead the way but Alex, can you keep tight up behind me, please? I might not be able to swing my axe in there, so I might need your sword as backup."

Alex stood behind him with his shield held forwards protecting his side and his sword held out over Jamie's shoulder, ready to thrust it into the head of anything that appeared.

With a shout of, "Ready boys!" he pushed his way into the bushes and disappeared from view. The other knights followed close behind. Seconds later, there was a yell of, "Get it!" and the bushes shook violently. I heard more shouts and swearing from all around me and the bushes moved like they'd been caught in a strong wind, until eventually all went still.

We stood ready for anything, counting the seconds until the bushes moved, making us raise our weapons slightly, ready to fire.

A shout of, "Ian's coming out" went up. It made us breathe a sigh of relief as he pushed his large body through the last branches and came out into the open.

"It's all clear," he said. "A few were stuck on the branches and a couple more were just getting through the gap. It was hard to get enough swing to get 'em but we managed. We've found the hole. It looks as if local kids have undone a bit of the fencing and peeled it back as a way of avoiding paying the entrance ticket. The rest are covering the gap, because there are a lot more wandering about out there."

He turned as more shouts sounded from behind him, followed by the unmistakable sound of an axe hitting soft flesh.

"It shouldn't be too hard to fix, but with the number of 'em out there, we need to do it quickly and preferably quietly. I'm sure the noise we made will be pulling them in from all around." Woody turned to Jon.

"Jon, you're our handyman. Can you go and check it out, please?"

With a, "Right you are then, cocker," he pulled an axe from his belt, walked down the ramp and holding it ready, followed Ian back into the bushes.

Jon had donned armour and fought alongside the knights ever since they'd found him, but on this occasion, Woody had asked him not to join them. Because of Jon's expertise in building and construction, he'd said his skills would probably be needed in other areas.

He emerged a minute later and walked to Woody's trailer, calling up to us as he rummaged around. "Not a problem. I'll fix the fence and reinforce it with some plywood sheets."

"How long?" called back Eddy.

As he picked up a few lengths of timber, he thought for a moment. "About half an hour if I do it by hand. If we fire up the genny, I can get it done quicker but we want to be quiet, don't we?"

He paused as an idea came to him. "If we can get to a builders' merchant, it might be a good idea to get some cordless drills. It would make some jobs a bit quieter and a lot quicker. Anyway, can someone give me a hand to get the gear moved and I'll get started?"

Noah, without asking, walked down the ramp and after Jon had shown him what to get, he followed him into the bushes, struggling under the weight of a sheet of plywood. We watched as the bushes near what we imagined to be the fence swayed and rustled as Jon worked to get the fence secured; an occasional grunt and the sound of a blade hitting soft flesh an indication that danger still lurked at the fence.

Eventually, a little more dishevelled and sweating than when they entered the bushes, the knights, Jon and Noah pushed their way back out into the sunshine.

"All done?" I asked.

Jon nodded, "Aye, spadge. That should hold 'em back, but the whole section of fencing is just chain link back there. It's not in bad nick, but if a lot of them push up against it, it could give way."

I pondered what he'd said for a few moments before replying with a sigh

"Well, it is what it is. I think once we've checked the whole perimeter for any more breached or weak points, can you come

43

up with a plan to improve it where necessary and a list of materials you'll need?"

"Yes, good plan," replied Woody. "But let's check the rest of the perimeter first. If everyone gets back on board, I suggest we go and find where it starts and then systematically work our way back."

The fence began in some woodland that ran alongside the River Avon. We didn't come across any more zombies and we checked the immediate area was clear, just in case the dense woodland was hiding some surprises. Woody asked for the knights to disembark and along with five more, me included, we followed the fence line, inspecting it as we went, while the two vehicles followed us slowly to provide cover and a place to retreat to if necessary.

The fence was mainly in good repair as the owners of the attraction, for good reason, needed to protect their property and also to stop those who thought they could avoid paying the entrance fee from sneaking in. A few areas were spotted where improvements could be made in the future and Jon noted them down in a small notepad he pulled from a pocket, but generally, we found no major issues. We realised to our chagrin, when we reached the gate, that we had failed to re-secure it when we'd used it the day before. The locking bar had been slid back into place after the padlock had been bolt cropped. But anyone could open it.

Woody summed it up, "No harm done, guys and no one's to blame. To be fair, we had a lot going on yesterday, so let's chalk it up to experience and forget about it."

The few other gates that allowed vehicles access were all secured with either padlocks or chains. Inspecting each one, the group had a discussion on the pros and cons of reinforcing them. The gates as moveable objects, even though they were locked, could be weak points. But if we reinforced them it could advertise our presence in the castle. It was a decision we decided to defer until later, because we still had a lot of perimeter to check.

Being in constant radio communication with the others gave us the confidence to continue our investigation. Waving at the ones on the ramparts as we passed, we carried on. The castle was in the middle of the large town of Warwick, so a lot of houses backed on to the perimeter, which in a lot of cases was a brick wall. Where we could, one person gave another a boost so they could look over the walls and inspect the area beyond. A few zombies, probably the previous owners, shambled around back gardens or could be seen in the houses. They presented no danger now, but we agreed that in the future it would be sensible to clear any houses that backed onto us and secure them. Not to extend the perimeter but keeping any of the undead further away would do no harm.

The fences eventually ended back at the River Avon, by the weir that had been constructed to power the mill. Remembering from our discussions earlier that the mill had been converted in the nineteenth century to provide electricity to the castle, once we'd checked the area, I asked Shawn if he wanted to do a quick inspection and see if he thought it could be used again.

Jumping down from the tractor, he followed me into the mill excitedly. The building contained a collection of machinery, all with signs on telling tourists what it had been used for. Shawn soon came to the conclusion that while it was all very interesting and he would love to 'play' with them, the mill contained no waterwheel, so there was no possibility of it being used to generate electricity. And the old fuel-powered generators that had been used as a backup would be noisy and inefficient and therefore were not worth attempting to get working.

He stated that, given time, he could use the flow of water through the mill race to construct a basic hydroelectric plant that would produce enough power to probably light the areas of the castle we needed. But why bother when we could use the large generator we'd loaded onto the trailer at Bickley barracks. By using the fuel we knew was in plentiful supply either in tankers or in all the vehicles that lay abandoned everywhere, we could generate enough power for all our needs. If the generator we had didn't have enough capacity, a larger one could probably be found locally. The fuel would eventually go bad but as that would take a year or two, it was something we didn't need to worry about for now.

Leaning on the rail that surrounded the mill race, both of us paused for a moment, mesmerised by the water rushing through the channel, when the radios in our pockets crackled into life.

"I can hear vehicles; they don't sound too far away," said a voice, the panic and urgency evident in the rapid and excited flow of words.

Rushing back outside, we found that the others had obviously heard the call, too, as everyone was obeying Woody and Eddy's urgent demands to get back into the vehicles.

"Back to the castle now. Let's lock it up tight."

Seconds later and with everyone in the trailer hanging on tightly, both vehicles sped up the pathway that led to the entrance blocked with the van.

CHAPTER SEVEN

As soon as the van was pulled back across the entrance, everyone disembarked and with both Eddy and Woody shouting commands and directing us, we all ran up the staircases and positioned ourselves around the castle walls.

Both sergeants were last on the walls. They'd removed the machine guns from the mounts on both vehicles and, struggling under the weight of the guns and an ammunition box containing the belted rounds for them, as well as their own personal weapons, they ran up the steps.

A bellow of, "QUIET!" from Eddy shut us all up.

The sound of multiple vehicle engines could easily be heard now. Noises echoed off the walls around us. They weren't far away at all, but it was hard to discern exactly which direction the noises were coming from.

I stood tense, holding my weapon ready, my mind whirling at all the possibilities. Were they friendly? If not, would we soon be defending our sanctuary from others who wanted to take it away from us?

The engine noise died down. Had they stopped? Had they moved on?

Five minutes later, my radio broadcast again. "I can see what looks like an armoured car coming through the grounds," Becky's voice shouted through the radio. She, along with two others, had run to the walls on top of the mound and from the high vantage point, they could see further than us.

Woody's voice immediately responded, "Keep reporting. We need to know what you can see."

"I can see a lorry now. It's green and looks the same as the ones the soldiers had on the motorway."

Craning over the ramparts from my position on the highest tower, I tried to see anything at all. But I was at the far end of the castle, so even from my high position I couldn't see past the mound where Becky was.

"They've stopped! Someone's looking at us through binoculars. I can see him standing on top of the armoured car," she reported, her voice rapid and high pitched with nerves.

"Wait…he's waving. I can't make out who it is, though."

"Hold on, Becky," Woody responded. "I'm on my way."

From my position, I saw him run down the steps from the ramparts and sprint across the courtyard and climb the path that led to the mound.

Before he could get there, Becky gave us another update. "I think I can see another lorry and a tractor coming up behind them as well."

Willing the radio to give me more information, I watched from a distance as Simon reached the walls above the mound.

Seconds later, distant cheers and shouts of joy reached me. The radio in my hand broadcast. Woody's voice, this time sounding joyous and laughing, and still breathless from his run across the castle grounds, came though the speaker.

"It's Captain Hammond and his men and and Fuck me! It's bloody Willie Beedie, if I'm not mistaken as well, driving a tractor."

I let out a whoop of delight. All along the walls everyone else was doing the same.

I couldn't believe it. All those days ago when we met them and traded information, guns and food on a deserted M5 motorway, we'd told the captain about our plan and about how Willie's farm would be a good place to seek shelter, if need be. Never thinking when we parted in all the chaos and death that was rampaging across the entire globe that from our chance meeting, our paths would ever cross again.

Barely audible over the noise of celebrations, I heard Woody ask for someone to move the van as they were heading in, and for everyone to leave their posts and meet on the courtyard.

I had to slow my headlong rush down the stairs as I almost tripped and fell in my eagerness to reach the courtyard. Smiling faces met and hugs were exchanged as we waited for them to appear. As Marc climbed into the van and pulled it away from the arch, Becky joined me, all smiles. I put my arm around her as we all crowded around the entrance.

First to come into view was the armoured car. The soldier manning the machine gun in its turret was pumping his fists like an overexcited trucker. Next came two lorries both 'up armoured' with familiar looking wedges and steel sheets fixed all around them. The sheets were dented, scratched and in places coated with blood and gore that bore witness to the events of the journey they'd undertaken. The drivers and passengers were leaning out of the windows, hammering their fists in celebration on the metal of the doors.

Both dogs got caught up in the excitement as well, bouncing around with their tails wagging furiously and added their barks to the celebrations.

Finally, and to the biggest cheer from all of us onlookers, including those who'd not met him yet, only knowing about him from the stories told of our saga so far, came Willie. Beaming and waving madly, he drove his heavily adapted tractor and trailer into the courtyard.

Marc pulled the van back across the archway and jumping from it, joined the rest of us.

Captain Hammond was the first to step from the vehicles and was quickly joined by his sergeant, who'd been driving the armoured car.

Both Woody and Eddy walked up to the captain, smartly came to attention and saluted the officer crisply. The captain returned the salute and smiling, extended his hand and shook both of theirs warmly in turn.

Any conversations were lost in the hubbub of laughter, yells of delight, barking and general merriment that filled the courtyard as the two groups combined into one.

Willie, I noticed, was standing on the high wheel arch of his tractor, his head turning and his eyes scanning the milling crowd of people. Then he spotted her.

Maud was standing in the ornate stone, open-sided entrance to the Great Hall, her face displaying a small smile. She locked eyes with Willie. By now, all our group had heard about what happened when they'd said farewell to each other at Willie's farm on the moors. Slowly, as if knowing something important was going to happen, one by one, we all fell silent.

Hesitantly, she slowly walked down the few steps of the entranceway and across the courtyard. Willie, seeing her approaching, clambered down from his tractor and made his way to her. Stopping a few paces apart from each other, we all watched as they both stood staring at each other.

Maud spoke first, her voice quiet and trembling slightly, "Willie, why are you here? You told me you wouldn't leave the moors."

Willie went red with embarrassment and looked at the floor, shuffling his feet. His mouth kept opening and closing as the beginnings of sentences started but faded as soon as the first mumbled word emerged from his lips.

Coming to a decision, he raised his head and stood upright. Staring her straight in the eyes he spoke gently, "Och, Maud. And I meant every word I said. That was, until you left and then suddenly everything seemed empty and without purpose." He waved towards Captain Hammond. "Even before I found that lot, I knew I'd made a mistake in not coming with you." He paused as if again thinking what to say. He stood staring at her silently for a long time.

As she returned his stare, a tear formed in Maud's eye and slowly ran down her cheek. Seeing this, a smile came to his lips and he continued.

"I'm too old to beat about the bush. Maud, you are the most attractive and the strongest woman I've met, and I was a fool to let you go before. If you'll have an old soldier who's grumpy and set in his ways, I would be honoured if you would allow me to court you and get to know you better."

Maud blinked in surprise at what she was hearing, but as she absorbed and truly understood the words, she burst out crying, her face displaying pure joy as she flung herself into his arms. He hugged her back fiercely as he lifted her up and held her tightly against his body.

The courtyard burst into spontaneous applause and cheering. I looked around, smiling at Becky as I clapped and shouted myself, and she was smiling and wiping away the tears that streamed down her face. Putting my arm around her, I could also see that a few others were wiping away tears as well.

Eventually, he gently put Maud back down. Becky and I, along with everyone else gathered around the beaming, very happy looking couple. Maud suddenly looked shocked. "I've forgotten about Sarah!' she blurted out. "She's asleep, but all the noise we've been making must surely have woken her up."

Nicky's pregnancy seemed to have put her maternal instincts on high alert, and because she was banned from any heavy lifting by the rest of us, she'd happily taken over some of the baby care duty from Maud. She put a hand on Maud's shoulder.

"Maud, don't worry, I'll go. If she's awake she wouldn't want to miss the party now, would she?" She turned and pushing gently through the gathered throng, walked towards the Great Hall.

The barking of the excited dogs echoing off the walls and the noise we were all making made me realise with a start that we'd forgotten our plan to keep quiet and not attract any unwanted attention from the potentially thousands of zombies roaming around in the local area.

Raising my hands in the air and shouting for quiet, I eventually got everyone's attention.

"I hate to break this up," I said, smiling, "but we were meant to try and keep quiet around here." Pointing to the main castle, I continued, "Can we all take this inside, folks?"

Fifty-two people and two dogs went inside to join Nicky and baby Sarah.

Our group now unbelievably numbered fifty-four; and two dogs.

CHAPTER EIGHT

The grandeur and impressiveness of the Great Hall momentarily quietened the new arrivals as they filed into the room. They stared around opened mouthed at the scale of the room with its weapon-covered walls and huge fireplace bracketed by windows that stretched upwards towards the high ceiling.

Taking advantage of the momentary quiet, I raised my voice and walked to the centre of the room with my arms held out in a theatrical gesture.

"Welcome to Warwick Castle," I said, smiling. "I know we all have a hell of a lot to talk about, but first of all, can we sort out security arrangements? We already have plans in place, but it would seem prudent to get all the new arrivals up to speed and in agreement. As your arrival has just proved, we just don't know what's going to happen from one moment to the next, so we all need to be on the same hymn sheet, so to speak."

There was a general murmuring of agreement and heads nodded. The new arrivals looked towards their captain, who walked over to me, but before he could speak, Charles, the vicar, walked into the middle of the room and raised his hands, appealing for the quiet to continue.

The soldiers and Willie all stared open mouthed at the sight of an elderly man adorned in the typical black shirt and white dog collar of his calling, but with the addition of a tactical vest over it stuffed with magazines, and a rifle on a sling over his shoulder.

"Before we begin, would you allow me to say a short prayer of thanks for the arrival of more people into our midst? I hope you don't mind."

Charles had, in the short time he'd been with us, become an integral part of our group. Always willing to help, not once despite his advancing years had he shirked any duty. He continued with the pastoral care that he'd administered before to his parish. He was not evangelical about religion and was always sympathetic and supportive with all he spoke to. He'd started giving a short prayer of thanks before meals which were more of a report on activities completed and others planned. Delivered with cheerfulness and humour, even though I was not religious, they were a pleasure to listen to and the obligatory 'Amen' at the end came naturally to everyone.

Bob and Jim both said that the work he'd done in their village community was fantastic, and his light-hearted and cheerful sermons attracted a lot of people to his small church. The pub in the village was another centre of the community and he was often in there, talking and laughing with the locals as he kept an eye on his flock and enjoyed a pint or two.

When he'd finished officially welcoming everyone, we got down to business.

"Sergeant Wood," began Captain Hammond, "why don't you start by giving us all a tour of the place and show us what you've achieved so far? I can then report to the Admiral of the Fleet and update him on the suitability of this place."

"Admiral?" I asked in amazement. "Have you contacted the fleet in the Solent?"

"How…how do you know about them?" he replied immediately, his voice full of curiosity.

So I told him about our brief contact with Graham and Arthur and what they'd picked up on the radios and their plan to sail their boats there. In return, he told us about their contact with them, using Willie's ham radio. Having the information confirmed gave us all another boost and my mind started racing as I imagined all the scenarios that might occur.

I started asking the Captain questions, but he didn't have any answers. All he knew was what he'd just told me, so I had to curb my curiosity and deal with the matters in hand: giving the new arrivals a tour of our castle home.

An hour later, a very impressed Willie, Captain Hammond and his men gathered back in the Great Hall. As we'd been touring the castle, they'd told us about their journey. Following the route they'd taken a few days before, their only dicey moment was when they'd encountered a huge horde heading towards them along the motorway. They were strung out over miles of road and not packed close enough to be a problem. So they'd decided to seal themselves in their vehicles and keeping their foot to the floor, smash through them. For mile after mile, the vehicles in tight single file formation had cleaved through thousands upon thousands of zombies that heedlessly kept walking into their path. There were one or two nervous moments when the weight of the corpses began to slow them down, but they kept pushing on, relying on the power and weight of the vehicles to defeat the undead. He described the destroyed still smouldering roadblock of vehicles under a motorway bridge, which remained a mystery to him, until we told them about our adventures and the sad loss of Daniel to the scum who'd set it up.

Becky, Eddy and Maud hadn't been idle while the tour had been taking place and had, with many willing hands, organised more rooms for everyone to use as private quarters. The suites of rooms the castle rented out to tourists would be the most comfortable. When we returned, they showed everyone the rooms they'd been allocated.

By universal agreement, Nicky and Chris, our expectant new parents, were given one. We insisted Maud take one of the apartments and she went all red with embarrassment, but didn't disagree when Eddy asked her, with a twinkle in his eye, if he should knock Willie off the list as having a place allocated to him.

We decided the other apartment should be taken by one of the families with kids, who could all be easily accommodated in it. Lots would be drawn as the fairest way of choosing who would take it. The multitudinous other rooms could easily accommodate all of us and leave many others for us to use as communal areas. We had a good supply of sleeping mats and airbeds that we'd got from the camping shop. We also put beds and mattresses on our ever-growing list of items required, because in the long term, they'd be a lot more comfortable.

While we'd been touring the castle, the sergeants, Willie included, discussed and agreed where to position the extra heavy weapons the soldiers had brought with them. They had GPMGs; general purpose machine guns, light machine guns, similar to those they'd already given us, and some fifty-calibre machine guns which, if mounted around the walls, would provide enough firepower to decimate any threat, both living and dead, that might want to try and take the castle from us. They'd also brought with them from the armoury at Imjin barracks an eighty-onemillimetre mortar. All the sergeants got very excited at this. If it was positioned in the centre of the castle courtyard, it would enable the mortar to lob its bombs over the castle walls accurately at any target within a three-hundred-and-sixty-degree arc; that was, once ranges had been spotted and marked all around our location. The mortar could fire both high explosive and illumination rounds, of which they had a fair supply of both.

I was trying not to get overexcited and overconfident when I saw what was being planned. It might all have seemed over the top and overkill, but as Eddy explained, there was no point them sitting in the lorry, and as we had the equipment, we might as well get it set up ready for use. I reminded him of the conversation we'd had about his plan to turn the castle into an armed camp, with machine guns mounted on the walls and artillery to blast anything that came near to clouds of blood and guts, and how that was happening on only our second day there.

He blinked in surprise as he remembered our conversation and subconsciously patted the pocket where he still had the lone shotgun cartridge which he'd found on the floor of the farmhouse. He could remember saying that if he ever found himself reaching for it, then they were well and truly fucked.

"Someone's certainly looking after us, I reckon," he stated simply. "Maybe this luck we keep finding will run out, but while it's being offered, we need to grab as much of it as we can." Laughing, he finished with, "So, let's cross everything we have and hope it keeps up."

Woody joined us and pointed at his friend Eddy. "I think we can set all this lot up with Captain Hammond's men. He wants to use Willie's radio to contact this admiral, so can you get who you need and go and help, please, Tom?"

I called to Shawn, who was with the others either unloading the supplies we still had in the trailer or moving furniture around to wherever Becky or Maud wanted it. All the children were helping, too, and we'd promised them that as a reward later, we'd let them go and play in the large playground that had zip wires and climbing nets and large wooden climbing frames designed as castles. It was in an enclosed area near the stables entrance and we figured that with a strong adult presence to act as guards, we could use a vehicle to take them the short distance to it and let them have some fun.

Willie helped us set the radio up, running the long antennae wire up to a high point on the building, while Shawn moved a small generator from the bus and ran a power cable to it from where he put it outside.

Willie sat down in front of it and grunted with satisfaction when at the press of a button it lit up, indicating it had survived the journey.

Turning to the correct frequency, he relinquished his chair to the captain, who sat down and picked up the handset.

"Captain Hammond requesting contact from Admiral Walker–Jones."

He waited for one minute and then repeated his call. The set crackled and a few broken words came in response. Willie leaned over him and turned a few dials and pressed some buttons.

"Try again, laddie," he said. This time the response was slightly better but still not clear.

"I'll have to go and extend the antennae some more," Willie said, unfazed by the frustration I was feeling at it not working yet. He turned to Shawn. "Come and give me a hand. I have more wire in ma trailer. If we run it up the highest point we can, it should do the trick."

Twenty minutes later, the two men returned and told the Captain to try again. This time, to my relief, the answer came back loud and clear.

"Captain Hammond," said the voice through the speaker, "this is Admiral Walker-Jones. It's good to hear your voice again, please update me on your progress."

First, he described their journey and how they'd found a complete lack of any other survivors as they'd driven through over two hundred miles of the country. He gave a brief description of our group and how perfectly suitable Warwick Castle was for our purposes. He'd already told him about us earlier from the information Willie had given him, so he was familiar with our story.

"Captain Hammond," the admiral began when he'd finished, "I agree your location seems ideal. Could you pass on my messages of congratulations and thanks to your hosts. Their tenacity and ingenuity are an example to us all. The tales you told us of their adapted vehicles have got us all thinking and planning along similar lines for when the time is right to take the fight to them and start reclaiming our country."

The captain turned to me and smiled as he replied. "Some are listening, Sir, but I will certainly pass your message along." He then turned serious again. "How are your plans progressing?"

"More Royal Navy ships and submarines have arrived. Arriving civilian boats have slowed to a trickle, but we are still broadcasting our location continually, so we hope that more will make it. They are sheltering in our lee at the moment and we are trying to get around them all in our small boats to distribute what rations we can. I have ordered all domestically owned commercial cargo and container ships to join us in the Solent and we are emptying those that have already arrived of any useful cargo as we speak. Without dockside assistance, it is a labour-intensive job, but I have teams of sailors with cutting gear opening up and working through containers, tunnelling into them and transferring what they find as best we can.

"Contact has also been made with Navies around the world. The situation we are in is being mirrored by most. The survivors are gathering together and are desperately trying to get organised to ensure not just their own, but the survival of their nations. It's too early to say if there will be any joint action, but lines of communication are remaining open and any useful information is being shared."

He gave an audible sigh.

"This morning I dispatched patrol craft to investigate small local ports, harbours and villages to see if a location for a defensible beachhead can be discovered, but as yet, no encouraging reports have come in. On a more positive note the helicopter carrier ship has entered the channel and will be with us within hours. I can then start reconnoitring for a suitable place for the fleet to shelter. The Scilly Isles still look favourite, but until we get eyes on it, we won't know for sure.

"If we can be of any assistance, Sir, bear us in mind. We have proven vehicles and sufficient firepower to reach most places, I imagine. Once we have helped fortify this place some more, we will be in a good position here."

"Thank you, Captain. I am sure I will call upon you soon. There are still personnel trapped in a few bunkers and posts, as I told you before. All are reporting they are secure and have sufficient supplies to last for the time being, but at some point, we will need to try and rescue them."

He broke off or a few moments. "Unfortunately, I have other matters to attend to and must sign off. Can you keep this line of communication open at all times in case we need to contact you urgently?"

Captain Hammond turned and looked at us. Shawn replied straight away. "Yes, we can. All we need to do is keep the genny topped up."

"Yes, Sir," continued Hammond, "we can keep it open."

"Good. Captain, your orders are to help and integrate yourselves with the group at the castle. Prepare as best you can for when we will go on the offensive. You are a credit to your country and your uniform and can be proud of what you have achieved so far. Out."

The captain's face turned red with embarrassment at the praise his superior officer had given him, as he laid down the handset on the ham radio.

"Shall we get on with our jobs, then?" he said. "The sooner we get them finished the sooner we can find something else to do."

***

As the shadows began to lengthen and the day gave way to dusk, we gathered back in the great hall. The walls were now adorned with multiple machine gun posts and a mortar position had been constructed, the kitchen area was stacked with supplies and lines of camping stoves; the sleeping areas had been allocated and mattresses and air beds lay on the floors of the many rooms surrounding us.

Once the children had run off the last of their energy in the play area, they'd been coaxed to bed, and the rest of us, apart from the ones on guard duty, sat on one of the many chairs that had been arranged around the main fireplace and rested our aching muscles.

Fifty-four people and two very tired dogs settled down to spend another night in our castle.

CHAPTER NINE

Awaking as light began seeping through the blinds that had been lowered in the room that was once an office and now was our bedroom, it took me a moment to realise where I was. Becky lay beside me, beginning to stir herself and I looked across the large room to the open door that led to where Stanley and Daisy were hopefully still sleeping in the adjoining room.

All seemed quiet and peaceful. The airbed we were using had thankfully decided not to deflate in the middle of the night, as had happened to us in the past, leaving us to wake up on a hard floor with the aches to prove it. Carefully, I extricated myself from the sleeping bag and rolling of the airbed, stood up and softly walked to the open door to check on the kids. They were still asleep, so once again trying and failing to be stealthy, I put on some clothes and holding my boots in one hand and my tactical vest and weapons in another, I walked into the corridor and down the stairs and passageway that eventually led to the Great Hall.

Laughter from the kitchen area drew me to it. Willie and Maud were bustling about, chatting and laughing together as they filled kettles from bottles of water and set them on the camping stoves. I leant on the doorway and smiled at how happy and relaxed together they seemed. They could have been a happily married couple who'd been together for years and not just the one day it had been. Willie laughed at something Maud had said and putting his arms around her, kissed her on the cheek. My chuckling at the sight caused them to both jump back in embarrassment as they noticed me for the first time.

"Och, laddie," Willie said, smiling, "what ya doin' creeping around like that? It's enough ta make ma heart stop, ya gave Maud a proper fright."

"I was hardly creeping," I replied, still enjoying the fact I'd caught them cuddling like teenagers.

Maud recovered by telling us both to leave her alone and she would bring us some mugs of tea through when the kettles had boiled.

Aiming for the comfiest looking chairs in the Great Hall, we sat and waited in comfortable silence for a few minutes.

"Willie," I said eventually, "I'm really happy for both of you. And...."

"Ah, stop ya girly mumbling," he replied, trying to be severe. "Maud's had enough of the women fussing around her like chicks around a hen, telling her it was one of the most romantic things they've seen. All I did was speak my mind and tell her how I feel. Now, can we move on and talk about something else for a change?"

Maud brought us two steaming mugs of tea and while we waited for others to arrive, we talked about our plans for the day.

The main priority was to continue the work of securing the castle. Last night, Chris and Jon had drawn up and finalised a list of supplies they would need to permanently brick up the few entrances to the castle or to construct sturdy gates to allow us to still use them for either vehicle or pedestrian access. We also needed to improve the perimeter fences at the few weak points we'd identified yesterday. Finding an old directory in one of the offices and using a map of Warwick town we'd found, we located the nearest builders' merchant and the first task of the day would be to dispatch a strong force to secure it, if necessary, and take what we needed. We had a long list of other items we wanted to gather, including more food and a plan to visit the list of local gun shops we'd also located using the directory. The growing list proved that for us to be confident that we could made the castle as impregnable as possible, we'd have days or possibly weeks of work and many potentially dangerous trips around the area to complete it.

Slowly, yawning and stretching, our little community gathered, and another day began. Not many were needed to stand guard on the walls, as from a few vantage points, the whole perimeter could easily be watched. To their delight, the six children who were deemed old enough were included on the rota. They'd helped to keep lookout at the church and were always told to help when on the vehicles, so it was nothing they hadn't done before. Now, however, due to the size of our new home, the adults would most likely be further away or occupied with other tasks.

Eddy told us that when the children were on duty, he planned to have an adult on the walls with them at all times, walking between their allocated posts. We'd tell them this would be as backup if need be, but we also knew the adult would be able to keep an eye on them and make sure boredom didn't make them lapse on what was essentially a crucial, but inevitably, boring job.

Woody and Eddy taught the youngsters basic drill and parade discipline and formed the eager looking 'soldiers' into a squad, with those of us who'd gone outside looking on and smirking at how serious they were.

Their young faces could barely contain their excitement as they stood there, each with a pair of binoculars around their necks, a radio in their pocket, and their prized .22 rifles slung over shoulders; all listening intently, as both sergeants, using their best 'sergeant's' voices told them the importance of what they were being trusted to do and the consequences of not concentrating.

Captain Hammond joined in and walked crisply on to the parade ground to receive smart salutes from both sergeants, and more exuberant, but not as neat ones from his new recruits. Then he told the sergeants to dismiss them so they could commence their duties.

The youngsters raced off to their posts. The adult chosen to join them set a more sedate pace.

Not knowing what to expect when we ventured out for the first time, we planned the mission carefully. The best vehicles we had were the armoured car, the tractors and trailers and woody's land rover. Chris told us that he expected the builders' merchant to have forklift trucks and hopefully a crane lorry, which if we could find their keys, as we had at the farmers' supply shop, would make loading easier.

The knights were our close quarters experts, so they were included in the party, along with half the soldiers. The rest of the soldiers stayed behind, because until the civilians were trained, they were the only ones who knew how to operate the machine guns we'd positioned around the walls. Out of the rest of us, we decided that ten would go, with everyone else staying at the castle.

The builders' merchant was only five minutes' drive away under normal conditions, so we thought the radios should still work, which would enable us to communicate easily. There was a lot of joking and banter to hide the nerves everyone was feeling at once again going out to fight the zombies we knew were out there. I was in the group chosen to go, and we all piled into Woody's Land Rover, Shawn's tractor and the armoured car, once again driven by Sergeant Geoff Gallon, with Captain Hammond beside him.

Once the van had been moved from its blocking position, with a final wave, we set off. Approaching the first gate, we could see a few zombies beyond it; not enough to worry us, but they were there, nonetheless.

Ian, Geoff and Jamie stepped from the rear of the armoured car and sliding the locking bar, opened the gate. We'd decided that it would be best for them to travel in that vehicle because it saved opening the rear of the trailer and deploying the ramp, if only a few of them could deal with what was out there. Standing aside for the vehicles to drive through, they made sure the gate was secure again, while we leant over the trailer sides, spears held ready to kil the few that staggered towards us.

The main entrance gate to the carpark was still closed. We could see more zombies beyond it, but none were close, so we were through and the gate secured again in no time.

The zombies that we'd just killed and those we dispatched yesterday must be getting in somewhere. We needed to find the hole in the fence or whatever they were using and fix it. I made a mental note to bring this up with the others later.

Shawn had the map, and with Louise in her normal spot beside him, they led the way. The route would take us through the centre of Warwick to an industrial estate just over the river. The road was littered with the usual and not unexpected mess of abandoned and wrecked cars, but Shawn was now an expert and easily picked the right path through them.

Until now, we'd avoided driving through any large towns, and we realised we'd done the right thing when we came upon places teeming with the undead. Shawn was forced to ignore the comfort of his passengers in the trailer and with his foot to the floor, he had to smash the plough on the front of his bucket through them.

In the trailer, all I could do was hold on as it bounced and rocked along the road packed with the dead. Looking back, the long, body-strewn path we cleared was soon filled with those he'd failed to hit as they turned and followed us. With dismay, I knew that as our objective was not far away, there would be too many for us to hold back when we tried to get what we needed. I reached for my radio and sat down on the floor of the trailer.

Knowing everyone, including those we'd left behind in the castle, was on the same channel, I spoke. "Guys, have you seen how many are out there? I think even with every gun firing, we'll struggle to hold them back. Anybody got any suggestions, other than turning around and heading back?"

Louise replied, "Shawn says that he's managing to smash through this lot, so as long as he can keep his momentum up, why doesn't he make a few passes through the town and keep thinning them out?"

I thought about the proposal, but it was the 'keeping the momentum' bit that worried me. If something happened, we could find ourselves in the same situation we had back at the barracks; jammed up against and unable to get through the thousands that faced us. That idea did not appeal to me one bit.

."Geoff's suggesting leading them away as they did at the church," said Hammond. "There might be a lot more we haven't seen yet, and he tells me it worked there."

That was a far more appealing plan. We'd all heard about how, when they'd first arrived at the village to help Bob and Jim find their families, they'd used the van to lead away the throng that surrounded the church.

"Shawn " I asked, "can you check the map to see if there's an easy way back? I don't fancy the risk of getting stuck if we can avoid it."

There was a pause while he and Louise were trying to find a route, then Louise spoke on the radio.

"Yes, if we carry on for about a mile after the town, we can loop back via the next motorway junction."

I mentally pictured the route from my knowledge of the area and knew it would work. Not needing to ask any more, with those in the other vehicles replying that it was worth a try, I put the radio back in my pocket, stood up again and clung to the side of the trailer as Shawn continued creating his gory trail of destruction.

Passing the builders' merchant, Shawn slowed slightly so we could study the place. It seemed perfect and was full of everything you'd expect the business to have, including a crane lorry parked in the middle of the locked and empty looking yard. Chris stood next to me, staring at it as we passed.

"Bonus," he said, smiling. "It looks as if the lorry was already loaded ready for the morning's first run. I couldn't see exactly what it was loaded with, but it definitely had some blocks and sand on it. If we can find the keys for it, we could just load whatever else we need and drive it back."

"I hope so. I can't imagine this'll get rid of all of them, so we aren't going to want to hang around," I added.

The crowd of zombies thinned out the further we got out of the town, making Shawn slow the pace to ensure the thousands following us kept up. With the leading edge of them yards from the armoured car at the rear of our convoy, we crawled along, reaching over the side and stabbing any that got close as we passed them, until at a traffic island, Louise told us Shawn would pick up the pace once we knew they'd followed us when we turned.

When we'd confirmed the undead mass was following us, Shawn sped up and our little convoy soon left them behind and in no time they were out of sight around a bend. Louise kept calling direction changes for everyone's benefit as Shawn drove the tractor back toward the M40 motorway. We'd crossed over it on our journey to the castle. From memory, I hoped it was still clear and only littered with the usual spaced-out abandoned cars and lorries we'd passed most of the way on our long journey up the M5.

I smiled as Shawn broke traffic rules and regulations and drove towards the off-ramp instead of crossing the carriageway to join the correct side of the road. Even though the laws of the land didn't apply anymore, I could imagine him enjoying the chance to flout them as he changed through the gears, gaining speed to join the motorway for the short trip back to the exit for Warwick.

Minutes later, we were back on familiar roads and once again driving past the castle entrance.

The masses had indeed, as we'd hoped, followed our initial direction. Slow ones, or ones left damaged by our first trip through, still crawled and dragged their way along the tarmac, their simplified senses telling them that was the direction to keep following to find food. Shawn began weaving the tractor to drive over as many as he could while those in the trailer stabbed and thrust at any others in range of our spears.

Yells of encouragement came over the radio because the ones still in the castle could hear our engine noises as we passed and they'd been following our radio conversations, so they knew what we were doing.

Captain Hammond spoke on the radio, "Okay, chaps. This time get ready. Shawn," he instructed, "if you drive through the gate and into the yard, we'll stop at the entrance with the other two vehicles and be the blocking force. Once the knights have checked the yard, form up by the vehicles and act as close support. Everyone else not needed in the yard, form on me with weapons ready. Everyone clear on that and happy?"

It was what I'd expected him to say and no one disagreed. As the senior military person present, he, with his sergeants to help, would naturally be in command of any fighting missions we undertook. This was his first one, and he hadn't seen any of us in action yet. He'd heard about it, but not witnessed our capabilities yet and I hoped he'd be impressed by what necessity had taught us.

Without slowing down, Shawn smashed the tractor straight through the entrance gate, which buckled and crashed back on its hinges with a sharp crack and the screech of breaking metal.

Driving once around the large rectangular yard, he stopped next to the lorry. In no time, we'd opened the door and deployed the ramp.

By the time the knights had walked down the ramp, Ian, Geoff and Jamie had got out of the armoured car and jogged over. We could tell the place was deserted, the open-sided sheds and the shuttered office and showroom building telling the story of a business that never opened on day one of the apocalypse, and never would again.

Once the knights had checked everywhere in the yard and shouted the all-clear, I joined Chris. They followed us as we headed straight for the shop door. There was no time for subtlety, so in seconds we'd cut off the padlocks to the shutters, pulled them up and used a sledgehammer to smash the front door in.

The shop area was dimly lit by skylights on the ceiling and we wasted a few seconds standing there, waiting for our eyes to adjust enough to see.

"Ian, Jamie," Chris said, "come with me while I find the lorry keys. Tom, you've got the list, see what you can find in here until we get back." As they disappeared through a door usefully marked with an office sign, I pulled a list from my pocket and called out items as we spread through the shop area. Getting a wheelbarrow from a display, we soon filled it with cordless drills, lengths of chain and other items that Chris had correctly assured us would be standard stock items for any builders' merchant. There was even a cement mixer which we filled with items we grabbed as we rushed about the shop.

The increasing level of fire outside was an unnecessary reminder to work fast.

With a shout of, "Got them," Chris ran past us and went outside. We grabbed a last few armfuls of items and followed, me pushing the wheelbarrow and Dave struggling with his sword, shield and a rifle on his back, dragging the cement mixer.

"Chris, how many of us do you need?" I asked.

"You and I should be able to do this," he shouted as he unlocked the lorry, jumped in and started its engine.

The knights didn't need telling twice and ran towards the smashed gates of the entrance and the continuous firing. Once I'd pushed the wheelbarrow up the ramp and helped Dave with the cement mixer, he ran to join them.

Chris had his foot fully on the accelerator of the lorry as he built up the air pressure as quickly as possible to get the pressure up in the brakes. As soon as he was satisfied, he jumped from the cab to the bed of the lorry, carrying a box. At first, I was mystified as to what it was, but it soon became apparent it was the remote control for the crane, as he placed the strap hanging from it around his neck and pressing a lever, raised its boom.

"I'll just get rid of what we don't need and then we'll find what we want," he shouted. Manipulating the crane, he picked up a pallet, and with a swing of the boom, he unceremoniously dropped it from a height and smashed its contents onto the yard. It looked like roof tiles. Two more smashed pallets later, he leapt from the lorry and joined me.

It sounded as if all the guns were firing, including the heavy machine gun on the armoured car. Looking towards the entrance, I could see the knights standing in line firing their guns, although not yet engaging any zombies hand to hand. I had to assume all was, if not contained, then at least under control. Shawn and Louise stood on the wheel arches of the tractor, with their guns held ready, keeping a good all-round lookout for any surprises.,

Now Chris was brandishing another set of keys. "Right, let's find the forklift. A couple of packs of blocks, timber, some plywood and a pallet of cement should do it. Can you drop the sides of the lorry, Tom?" Struggling briefly with the clips that secured the hinged lorry sides in place, I waited as he ran off in the direction of an open-sided shed.

I was impressed with his competence, because it took him no time at all to find the forklift and operate it. Pushing it to its maximum speed, he rushed around the yard, filling the space he'd made on the lorry with various packs and pallets, double stacking a few of them, until with a yell of satisfaction, he jumped from the forklift and together, we lifted the sides of the lorry back into position.

"You got everything else on the list, mate?" he asked as we took the straps he'd grabbed from the lorry's cab and threw them over the load to secure it.

I nodded, "Yes, and more. I grabbed any extra stuff I saw, since we were here anyway." I pointed to the lorry. "You get in and I'll go and tell them we're ready." I winced at the sound of firing. "I don't think they'll hear us over the radio." He slapped me on the back in acknowledgment and ran towards the open door of the lorry.

Grabbing my rifle from where it rested on its sling over my shoulder, I sprinted towards the gate and the firing. Zombies were approaching from all directions in large numbers. The gunfire was keeping them at bay, but I could tell from the trail of bodies that they were getting closer. The knights looked out of place in full armour as they fired their modern weapons. It looked as if someone had made a dreadful historical error when writing a movie script. Hundreds of empty bullet casings littered the floor, indicating how heavy the firing had been.

Captain Hammond and his sergeant were walking the perimeter he'd set up and encouraging them all. Occasionally raising his rifle and firing when needed, it took the captain a few seconds to notice me standing there waving at him. I gave him the thumbs-up and waited for him to acknowledge before running back to the yard.

Shawn and Louise had seen me give the captain the signal and were already back in the tractor. I indicated for them to pull forward and get as close to the knights as possible. I had a feeling that when they disengaged and the fire reduced, the approaching tide of the undead would be unstoppable. The sound of whistles blowing split the air and immediately the volume of fire decreased as the knights responded to the signal to withdraw to the safety of the vehicles. Running as fast as the weight they were carrying would allow, they ran towards the open rear of the trailer. Steadying them, I helped them up the ramp and as soon as the last one was in, I pushed on the ramp while they pulled the ropes inside to get it onboard, and we slammed the rear door shut. Dashing to the lorry, I climbed into the passenger seat and holding my weapon out of the open window, I waited for the convoy to start moving.

Sitting in the raised cab, I watched the last soldiers get into the rear of the armoured car and close the door. Then Captain Hammond's voice came over the radio.

"Shawn, when we move, can you take the lead and do the same as before? I'll bring up the rear and if Chris follows Woody, we can both cover you." It made sense, because although the lorry had high ground-clearance and heavy-duty fenders, it wasn't armoured like all the other vehicles were, making it the most vulnerable. Knowing those at the castle would be receiving as well, he continued. "Can you get ready with the van, please? We should be back in five minutes. Please acknowledge."

Multiple voices from the castle replied, telling us the van was already running and waiting. Our firing would be clearly audible to them and they must have known something was happening when the level reduced, the response was so quick. With the engine revving, Chris followed Shawn as he left the yard and waited for Woody to turn his Land Rover around, before following him closely.

I knew that Warwick was a large town that was growing bigger by the year, with hundreds of new homes being built annually to house those who wanted to leave the city to live a more 'rural' and genteel life offered by the pretty towns that surrounded the urban sprawl of Birmingham.

Looking ahead, I could see that thousands more zombies were still appearing from all directions. The obvious reason was that once again, with all the gunfire and engine noise, we were now, and always would be, the noisiest and most irresistible target around. I looked again at the masses being destroyed by Shawn's plough and the hundreds we had just re-killed with bullets, and wondered what would happen if they managed to breach the perimeter walls and fences and surround us in the castle. We would, of course, be safe behind its walls, but we could also find ourselves trapped, with not enough bullets to deal with the population of just one small town in England, and with no hope of restocking our supplies of food or other necessities. A worrying thought.

Ten minutes and many destroyed zombies later, we secured both gates, using our recently acquired chains locked with padlocks to add more strength to them, and drove into the courtyard.

After a brief separation, we were again fifty-four and two dogs.

CHAPTER TEN

The children were still guarding the walls, with the adult who was keeping an eye on them reporting that they were all continuing to take the task seriously. The amount of gunfire that had echoed around the castle walls was probably a better reminder than anything else for them not to slack in their duties.

Everyone's relief at us all being back safe after hearing so much gunfire was evident as we gratefully accepted mugs of tea and shrugged out of our equipment in the Great Hall and discussed what we would do next.

The main priority was to secure our weak points. Chris and Jon were tasked with leading the project, because they were the ones with building experience and we told them they could have as much manpower, or woman power, as they needed.

Chris wanted to seal off any entrances we didn't want to use with brickwork, and Jon was confident that with what we already had and our newest supplies from the builders' merchant, he could construct heavy-duty gates on the others. This led to a debate on how many entrances we needed. Currently, the barbican entrance was guarded by the sturdy portcullis and blocked by my Volvo, parked at an angle in it, its front and rear pressed up tightly against the stone sides. We'd been using the archway that had been opened in the walls of the castle in more recent times. Chris proposed an idea; if he blocked up the archway and put a doorway in it for pedestrian access if we decided it was necessary, then the barbican entrance would be the best to use as the main entrance. After all, it already had the formidable portcullis, which we could raise easily. If Jon could make a new gate to replace the one that had once stood behind the portcullis in times past, the castle would revert to its original design when entrances were always the weakest points, and apart from a few sally ports, were normally limited to just one that was heavily guarded and fortified.

It was, after all, what the barbican entrance was, originally having a drawbridge over the moat as the first line of defence and then the portcullis with probably more than one gate behind that. Archers and soldiers could rain death, using arrows, rocks, boiling, tar, sand or water upon any attackers. If the initial defences were breached, they had to fight through the heavily fortified barbican with its murder holes in the ceiling and multiple arrow slits for the defenders to use.

As a group, we pondered and discussed the proposal. Shawn raised a valid point when he asked if the entrance would be wide or high enough for our vehicles to use. Three of us volunteered to investigate and, armed with a tape measure and after some careful calculations, we decided that they would; just. The proposal was agreed when we decided that if we had to get out in an emergency, our vehicles would have the power to smash through the newly blocked-up archway, opening another escape route.

Decision made and with both jobs being priority, we wasted no more time. Chris drove our newly acquired lorry around the courtyard, using the crane to deposit its contents where they were needed. Jon set up an area as a workshop and, using some timber and plywood sheets, he made a workbench. The most labourintensive job was laying the blocks, because people needed to work together, both mixing cement and carrying and laying the heavy concrete blocks. Jon said he only needed a few to help him construct and fix the gates.

Generators were set up and we allocated people roles and set to the task with a purpose, while trying to keep noise to a minimum. We hoped the noise of the cordless drills we'd got for Jon would be contained within the castle walls, but as they were essential to complete the task as quickly as possible, we had little choice in the matter.

Fortunately, water was still flowing from the taps in the castle, so we formed chains and passed buckets from hand to hand to make the mortar. We'd decided not to use it for drinking ,as the treatment plants would obviously not be working, but for as long as it lasted, it could still be used to flush the toilets in the place and be used for washing, etc. If, or more likely, when it stopped flowing, we would just have to come up with an alternative, but for now it was, and that was good enough for us.

Sweating in the sun, everyone who wasn't on guard or babysitting duty mucked in and helped. Throughout the rest of the day, the wall in the archway slowly gained height as blocks were passed from hand to hand and laid on beds of mortar. Jon made a frame out of lengths of timber and a doorway was created in the structure.

The wooden gates were quicker to construct. Using heavy duty strap hinges from the merchants, he soon had the framework of the gates in place and attached to the walls of the barbican. Once he was satisfied they were hanging correctly, he planned to add layers of timber to reinforce them. When he'd finished, he also wanted to add another angled gate to the front of the bridge that crossed the moat. He explained that it didn't need to be as sturdy or as high as the one he was making now, but it would keep any zombies away from the portcullis itself. It was a good idea, so we all told him to get on with it as soon as he'd finished what he was doing.

I found myself forgetting the world outside our walls as we laboured away. The hard, physical work occupied all my thoughts until I took a break to grab a bottle of water and looked around the ancient castle that had become our home. It was a truly stunning place which, once we'd finished, would be as impregnable as when it was first built almost a thousand years before. Sentries walked the walls as they had in ancient times; this time, though, instead of crossbows and spears, they carried modern assault weapons and could fire at any attacker from one of the many machine gun positions we'd created.

In place of the cannons and trebuchets that would once have lined the walls for defence, the soldiers had created a sandbagged emplacement in the middle of the courtyard, which housed the mortar they'd brought with them. This could lay down a far heavier and more accurate barrage than could any weapon designed before it. It was a clash of technology that somehow worked and did not look wholly out of place in such an old and historic complex.

Smiling at my thoughts, I finished my bottle of water and got back to work.

***

Hours later, we gathered back in the great hall. The work was almost complete. We were satisfied as we called it a day that what we'd already achieved was as good, if not better, than we'd originally expected. The van was still pulled in front of the archway, because it seemed prudent to leave it there until the mortar had set. The gates constructed by Jon and his team had been finished and passed our collective inspection. With the locking bars and bolts in place, they seemed strong enough to withstand a ramraid, let alone a horde of zombies.

Bellies full of the food produced by Maud and her helpers, we opened and passed around bottles of wine and beer and everyone drank, happy in the knowledge that fifty-two people were all a little safer now than we had been the day before.

The two dogs, both filthy from many incidents with the wet mortar, were banished to the floor.

CHAPTER ELEVEN

It was chiller and more overcast the next morning. There were no more weather forecasts, but we all agreed that it looked as if we were due for some rain.

Pulling on sweaters we soon knew would be discarded when the physical worked warmed us up, we organised ourselves into teams to complete the jobs for the day. Fewer people were needed for the work to complete the bricking up of the archway, so we turned our attention to the task of reinforcing the perimeter fence.

Jon busied himself preparing the tools and materials he wanted to take and then, after a final check of the notepad in which he'd written what needed doing, he asked for help to get it all on Woody's trailer, which also provided us with a safe vehicle to carry all the volunteers. Willie was driving his tractor this time as Shawn was still helping Chris with the brickwork. We drove through the barbican entrance and began the day's work.

Exhausted and hungry, we returned many hours later. Woody's trailer was empty of everything we'd loaded that morning. We'd had enough material to strengthen extra sections of the perimeter, although it probably didn't need it; but since we had the materials, while we were at it we thought it prudent. After all, we knew we could always scavenge more if necessary.

Following another collective meal and a few relaxing drinks, it didn't take any of us long to fall asleep that night.

Up early in the morning, we inspected the to do list that was continually being added to and altered and we planned the day. Now that we were confident that the security improvements we'd made to the castle, both inside and out, were almost completed, food and weapons were top of the list. We had ideas to improve security even further, but for now things were good enough.

The soldiers claimed that weapons and ammunition should be the priority, because even though they had many thousands of rounds and we could make many thousands more from the home loading supplies we'd got from the gun shop, we'd expended a lot over the last few days and getting as much as possible should be top of the list. We'd already identified and located the nearest gun shops from the directory we'd found and one or two were reasonably close. Others said that food should be the priority, because if we were besieged by countless zombies, it wouldn't be bullets that kept us alive behind the walls, but food.

Although we knew both proposals were of great importance, we didn't want to split our forces by pursuing different objectives. Our strength lay in numbers. After much deliberation, we decided to try and achieve both tasks in one trip. We'd located a local trade-only food warehouse that supplied local shops and businesses. We thought because the food would be on pallets, that would speed up the loading process, and it would be easier and quicker than raiding one of the many supermarkets in the town. After studying the map, we also realised that it wouldn't be a big diversion to get to the nearest gun shop. If it turned out to be similar to the gun shop in Newton Abbot, the stuff we could get wouldn't take up as much room as pallets of food, so hopefully, we'd be able to be squeeze it onto the lorries and trailers, along with the food. With everyone satisfied and in agreement, the planning was handed over to our military contingent.

Fifteen minutes later, Captain Hammond called us all together for a meeting. He proposed the largest expedition we'd undertaken to date, using the most vehicles and taking more people than any we'd ever done before. We'd be using both army lorries, the armoured car and Woody's Land Rover; in addition, he also wanted to include not only Shawn's tractor and trailer but our newly acquired crane lorry too. The theory being that if the warehouse was suitable, we could load up enough food in one go to last us for months, possibly even longer, saving the need and risk of venturing out again for food for quite some time.

On the way back, if it looked safe to stop, we'd find the gun shop and take everything we could.

It was a bold plan and even though we'd successfully completed similar missions, we hadn't undertaken one on this scale before. He said himself that we needed to be fully prepared and ready, because the bigger the mission, the bigger the potential cock-ups.

A little daunted by the idea, nevertheless we did all agree that is was worth trying and we got on with it.

Captain Hammond asked Maud to come up with a wish list for the food warehouse, so they could identify and prioritise loading the large quantity of foodstuffs and other items we hoped we'd be able to get. Shawn, Willie and I were tasked with adding protection to the lorry. We didn't have time to do a full job on it, but we thought that if we added some of the mesh panels we still had around the cab, and reinforced the front so it could smash through the undead without causing terminal damage, it would be better than nothing. Given more time, we could make it as impregnable as the rest of our vehicles, but if it travelled in the middle of our convoy it would be protected by the other vehicles.

Eddy, who was going to remain and guard the castle, selected who he wanted to stay with him. It was only fair that he should have first dibs with people, because if the castle wasn't left defended properly, none of us would want to leave our families and loved ones behind.

An hour of frantic preparations later, we were ready and those chosen to go boarded their designated vehicles. All the vehicles had been checked over and any necessary repairs carried out. Shawn made sure the petrol cutter was working, and the same for the other equipment we thought we might need to break into the locked areas of the gun shop. While he was doing that, others loaded extra guns and ammunition and a small supply of food and water, just in case. We waved to those staying behind and for the first time, we drove out through our newly fortified barbican entrance.

Becky stood beside me in the trailer. We'd had a brief 'discussion', with her calling me a sexist because I begged her to stay and take care of the children when she insisted on being included on the mission. She was confident that they would be looked after well by Maud, Eddy and the ten other adults chosen to remain and she told me that she was just as capable of killing zombies as anyone else, something she'd proved many times before. She also joked that we needed to include more women on the shopping trip, because if it was left up to the men, all we'd get was pallets of beer and boxes of crisps.

She did have a point.

With a final wave to our children back on the walls keeping guard, we disappeared from their view. Becky stood holding on to the side of the rocking trailer, her weapon over her shoulder and a pistol on her hip, the tactical vest she was wearing stuffed full of extra magazines. It was a look I thought I'd never see on her, but to be fair, I thought she looked sexy.

I moved closer and put my arm around to help steady her and whispered cheekily in her ear.

"Look at you all dressed up in your finest gear. I know I never say it often enough, but you look damn good, woman."

She just looked at me with raised eyebrows. Undaunted, I continued.

"And you say I never take you out. Here we are, off on a date without the kids. Don't you ever moan at me again, my darling, for not making an effort."

She rested her head on my shoulders, she knew I was just trying to take her mind off leaving the children behind and I think she appreciated it, but after a few moments of quiet companionship, she had to have the last word.

"Tom, if you think this is a date, I think you need to go and have a long, quiet word with yourself. Right now though, we're getting near the gate, so we'll have to discuss this later."

Fortunately, only a few zombies could be seen beyond the first gate. Maybe whatever gap or hole they'd used to get in before wasn't obvious to the hordes that filled the town. We still needed to find it, and it was on our growing list of jobs that needed doing, but for now it wasn't posing a great problem.

We were through the gate in minutes as once again a few knights climbed out of the back of the armoured car to unlock it. They waited until we'd all got through, then secured it and climbed back into the armoured car, which had pulled to one side to wait for them. The other gate proved to be a different matter altogether. Hundreds of zombies could be seen just beyond it. It didn't take a genius to work out that they were the ones that had followed the swath of destruction and noise we'd cut the day before when returning from the builders' merchant.

The noise of us approaching caused the nearest to turn and head in our direction.

Captain Hammond spoke through the radio. "Okay, chaps, I think this is the time to show me what you knights can do. If you form up by the gates and open them when you're ready, we'll drive through and thin them out a tad and then loop round and pick you up." Pausing for a moment, he continued, "Does that sound like a plan?"

Ian responded a few seconds later. He was in the trailer beside me. "Okay, lads, let's show the army boys what we can do. Grab your pikes and head to the gates."

Hinging back the door on the trailer, we pulled on the ropes to lower the ramp and passed the pikes to the knights when they'd all got out. They made their way to the gates, joining those that had left the armoured car.

Hundreds of zombies were crowding towards the gate, making it rattle and push against its locking bar. Even after all we'd seen and experienced, the sight was a daunting one.

Seven knights stood at the gates and began thrusting their pikes through the slats at the nearest heads. Bodies fell and soon began piling up in a macabre wall. More kept trying to crawl over the growing obstruction until their existence was ended by the sharp point on the head of the pike. Eventually, the pikes could no longer reach the masses beyond and the knights, sweating and breathing heavily, stepped back and surveyed the carnage they'd wreaked. Hundreds of bodies lay before them, but worryingly, hundreds more crowded in behind them.

Captain Hammond used the loudspeaker on the armoured vehicle to communicate this time. His voice boomed out. "Well done, chaps, great work. If you could open the gate and let us through now, we'll thin the others out. Hold the line at the gates and we'll be back with you shortly. Woody, can you stay back in the Land Rover to provide cover for them? If everyone could honk their horns to confirm you understand, we'll get on with it." Five horns blasted their reply and revved their engines.

Ian stepped towards the gate and removing his glove, turned the dials on the padlock to the right code to unlock it and unwrapped the chain from around the gate. The coded padlocks were chosen from the ones we'd got from the builders' merchant as the best to use. Remembering a four-digit code would be better than making sure the key didn't get lost or forgotten, causing potentially dangerous delays and problems when opening the two main gates to the castle.

After checking the other knights were in position and the vehicles were ready, he slid the locking bar back and straining against the weight of the few bodies that were caught on them, pulled the gates open.

Shawn was first through. Lowering the plough to scrape on the ground, he powered the tractor into the tangled pile of bodies. Corpses mangled together as the plough pushed them aside to form a monstrous corridor of death. Body parts ripped from corpses lay abandoned in his blood-smeared wake as the lorries followed, bouncing over any that fell back into their path from the piles Shawn had created.

Those of us in the trailer stabbed at any near us, but the wild, bouncing ride we were on made even standing up difficult, let alone using our spears accurately. Frustrated, I picked up a shotgun and started blasting away at the many targets that surrounded us. I considered the shotgun, with its spread of lead pellets, to be better than using my rifle, only necessary where accuracy was more important. Others in the trailer followed suit, including Becky, as Shawn ploughed through the undead, making the trailer rock and sway as he swerved through, trying to get as many as he could.

Heads turned into smoking messes of brains and bones as the heavy lead-filled cartridges ended the existence of more zombies. Looking back, I could see that the two army lorries weren't following in Shawn's tracks, but had spread out slightly on either side of him to widen the path of destruction created, like a team of snow ploughs clearing a road. Shawn's plough smashing through them was pushing destroyed and broken bodies aside into the path of the vehicles following. It made economical work as they destroyed the ones directly in front of them as well as hurling aside those pushed into their path. I hadn't heard this tactic being discussed so it must have been a good idea hastily thought up which was proving to work brilliantly, because now, we weren't just cutting a single path through them, but an entire swathe.

When the crowd thinned, Shawn used the whole width of the road to turn around and head back the way we'd come, the engine roaring powerfully all the while. The army lorries followed with the armoured car and the crane lorry. Passing the gate, I caught a glimpse of the knights standing with shields raised, hacking at the ones before them, while Woody and Steve fired over their heads from their elevated position standing on the seats of the Land Rover. The zombies had been thinned by us smashing through them, but they were still facing a large crowd. From what I could see, though, they were coping and no call for help came over the radio, so we continued.

Two passes later and with our vehicles coated in another layer of gore and sporting a few more dents, Captain Hammond radioed, telling us we'd done enough and that we should collect the knights from the gate.

CHAPTER TWELVE

The bodies had piled up again as the knights practised their deadly trade and Shawn was forced to use his plough to clear the gate once more. Woody reversed his Land Rover out of the way to allow him and the armoured car to pass straight through the gate and turn around to get the knights back on board.

Both machine guns on the armoured car and the Land Rover then laid down a withering level of fire to cover the knights as they, with a final thrust of swords, axes and maces, picked up their pikes and ran back to the vehicles.

On the trailer we all helped the exhausted knights climb the ramp, holding out arms and hands to help them the last few paces. And then taking their weapons from them, we handed them bottles of water and cloths to wipe their blood-streaked faces and armour. Shawn, driving a little more slowly this time, pulled back out onto the main road. We waited until Captain Hammond had closed and secured the gate once more as we stabbed and shot any that tried to get past us to reach him.

The food warehouse was on the same road, but further out of town than the builders' merchant we'd visited the day before, so once again we needed to drive through the centre of Warwick.

The road was littered with the results of our previous action but happily, the 'live' ones were not as numerous. It was impossible to know how many we'd dealt with, but the hundreds of corpses being picked apart by innumerable carrion birds fluttering away half-heartedly as we passed was a stomach-wrenching sight. We'd already led a horde of many thousands away and we didn't know how many more still roamed the town's suburbs and side roads.

I sighed. This was only one relatively small town of the many hundreds all over the country. If you included the cities, how many millions upon countless millions of zombies were roaming the land, searching for their next meal? It would be impossible to kill even a small fraction of them. The only hope for humanity was for small outposts of survivors such as ours to gather supplies and remain safe until hopefully, the undead started to rot and turn to dust.

Gathering supplies was the problem because that inevitably meant leaving our sanctuary to face and survive the terror that lived outside our walls.

The tractor lurched as it rode over bodies and smashed through the ones that Shawn could aim at. We tried to stab or shoot as many as we could when passing, because no matter how many millions more there were, one less was still one less. We breathed a sigh of relief when we drove into the food warehouse's large car park, just as we had when we'd raided the outdoors shop, and we saw it contained only a few awkwardly staggering figures. Most businesses hadn't opened on the first morning of the apocalypse, their staff or owners were already dead or far too preoccupied to worry about work. So, remaining empty and deserted, they contained nothing to attract the undead and had remained devoid of the masses that filled other places.

"Right then," announced Captain Hammond over the radio, once we'd driven a loop around the carpark to rid ourselves of its current residents. "If the lorries can get as close to the entrance as possible, the rest of us will form a defensive cordon. Knights, if you do the initial sweep of the interior, backed up by five others with guns, once you can give us the all clear, we'll get cracking."

The radios all crackled with affirmative responses before the vehicles started to shunt into position.

I joined the knights with four others at the shuttered entrance. Getting more adept with every break-in, the external security took no time at all to breach and with a wrench of a crowbar to the main door, we were in.

Ian took command. "Okay, ladies. Stick together and let's go up and down every aisle first." He pointed at what looked to be some offices that overlooked the interior of the building. "Then we check everywhere else out. Keep talking and calling out targets." He looked at the five of us standing there with our weapons ready. "You lot, as before, stay in the middle of our formation and when we need you, you'll be notified by Simon's high-pitched girly squeal of terror."

Simon was the only one not to dutifully laugh at his attempt at humour and retorted with, "Oi, Beaver, why don't you pick on someone your own size? Oh, I forgot, no one is as big and stupid as you."

With some more banter, the friends, seemingly relaxed and without a care in the world, checked their armour, hefted their shields and once more took the lead against the zombies. Aisles stacked high with pallets containing a huge variety of different goods stretched before us. I tried to take note of the location of everything, so that when we began working our way through the list Maud had given us, we could locate the items quickly.

***

Two hours later, we were still working hard under the direction of Becky, Louise and Victoria, who were all armed with lists, rushing around telling us which pallet to load next onto one of the hand-pump pallet trucks we'd found. Then we hauled them outside to another team who were ripping off the wrappings and passing boxes, cartons and sacks from hand to hand to load the lorries and trailer. The crane lorry had loaded itself and was now full of double-stacked pallets secured by lengths of rope.

The knights were standing guard and taking a well-earned rest after their earlier exertions. If they were needed again, then it was imperative they were as fresh as possible. Wielding their weapons and fighting in a shield wall was probably one of the most physically demanding things anyone could do. They were accustomed to it, though, and had trained regularly before the apocalypse started, knowing from doing re-enactments how much effort it took to fight for an extended period of time. But no matter how fit they were, they needed to rest their aching muscles so when they were recalled to the fray, they could once more fight to the best of their abilities. Everyone else on the mission was on collection and loading duties. None of us was far away and we could all be defending the perimeter within minutes if we needed to.

When Becky and Louise were satisfied that we'd procured most of the items jotted down on the list, they led teams of us dashing around the warehouse with large trolleys to load on other items they'd noticed and decided we could do with. We threw every item they pointed at into the trolleys and when they were full, we ran outside to empty them and fling it all in the lorries on top of everything we'd already loaded. When the radios broadcast the inevitable and not unexpected warning of, "Zombies! Everyone back to the trucks," no one hesitated, and pushing and pulling loaded trolleys, we headed outside.

Inevitably, they'd found us. Whether they were ones from earlier who had followed us or others who had been attracted by our noise, even though we'd tried to be quiet as possible, it didn't matter. They were there and in large numbers. With a final effort, we heaved the last items from our trolleys into the lorries and got on board ourselves. Our final act was to close the shutters on the shop to, if not secure it, then stop any wandering ghouls from inadvertently entering. The place still contained a large amount of supplies, so this was just common sense, because if we had to return, the last thing we'd want to do was to clear the place of any zombies first.

The captain had relinquished command to Becky at the warehouse and had been working just as hard as everyone else loading the lorries. Now the convoy was moving, he took over again.

"Good work, everyone," he announced needlessly. "Now the gun shop. Same drill as before. Once we gain entry, we will secure the perimeter and start loading up. We know what the priorities are, so concentrate on those first and if time allows, we'll look for other items that might be useful."

All of us knew what the priorities were. Basically, bullets, bullets and more bullets and if we could find them, more bullets. Ammunition for both rifles and shotguns had to be the priority.

Every time we left the castle we were burning through ammunition at a prodigious rate and even though we had a large supply in reserve, we knew that enough would never be enough until the last zombie in the country had been exterminated. Guns were one thing we had plenty of, after our raid on the last gun shop, coupled with what the soldiers had brought with them, but still, they were on the list as well. Our immediate need was not our only concern. We might to arm others beside ourselves and if the guns were there for taking, then take them we would. The contents of just a single gun shop would never provide what we wanted, but it was a step in the right direction.

The gun shop was in a small row of shops on a housing estate. Sandwiched between a café and a local convenience store, the double-fronted shop was shuttered and looked deserted. A few zombies attracted by the noise we were making shuffled into view as we positioned the vehicles. Stabs from our spears ended their existence as soon as they were in range. After a few radio calls, the vehicles eventually stopped, nose to tail with the lorry at the rear and Shawn's tractor at the front at an angle to create a solid barrier with a large protected space in front of the shop.

We waited for the captain, as he stood on the wheel arch of his vehicle, looking all around to assess the situation and issue his orders.

"Okay, guys," he began, "there looks to be nothing we can't handle, so I say we go for it. Those on guard, stay on the vehicles and get ready to take the stuff we pass up to you. We won't know until we get inside how much there is and how long it'll take, so stay sharp, everyone, and let's try to get this done as quickly as possible."

Opening the back of the trailer once more, we lowered the ramp. The back of the trailer was already piled high with a jumble of boxes, sacks and slabs of tinned food. While others broke into the shop, I and a few others began shifting what we had into a more organised stack to make room for what we hoped we could get.

Woody emerged from the shop a few minutes later and spoke to the ones waiting outside, "Right, let's form a chain and start passing it all out."

"How much stuff is in there?" I shouted down to him.

"We've opened the cartridge store and it has a fair amount in, not as much as there was at Newton Abbot, I've been told, but it'll do. We're still trying to break into the ammunition safe, but again, it's not that large so I don't expect it'll hold much."

"Don't forget the home-loading stuff," called Willie from beside me on the trailer.

Woody smiled at up at him. "I was just coming to that, Willie. Can you get in there and start sorting through the shelves? You know what you're looking for better than any of us and it might save some time." Willie nodded and strode down the ramp and into the shop just as the first slabs of shotgun cartridges started to get passed out.

Trying to remain as quiet as possible, we began using the silenced .22 rifles on the undead when they got close enough. We knew there must be thousands in the area, possibly making their way to us now. If we kept any noise we made to a minimum, it might delay them finding us for a time.

Alternating between firing at any zombies that came close enough and helping to pass and stack the growing pile of cartridges, I was distracted by a banging sound coming from above us. I searched for it, because I initially thought it might be a survivor trying to get our attention, but my momentary hopefulness ended when I saw the head of a zombie banging against the closed window of what must have been a flat above a shop two doors away. It was still above the protected area our vehicles had created, but I gave it no more thought since it couldn't harm us, and we had plenty of work to get on with.

Willie kept rushing in and out of the shop, carting carrier bags with the shop's name on filled with what I reasoned to be home-loading supplies and he stacked them in a corner of the trailer.

The work continued with a quiet but determined pace until Captain Hammond walked out of the shop carrying a large nylon bag which he slung into the back of a lorry. His face was dripping with sweat and he paused to take a long drink from the canteen on his belt before speaking to us all, "Can I have a few of you down to exchange positions with some of us? It's bloody heavy work and a few of us are flagging. Some fresh pairs of arms will keep the pace going and there's not much more stuff left to get loaded."

He smiled and nodded at our immediate and positive replies. "Thanks. I'll send one out at a time and if you can replace them, it will save us stopping the chain we've formed."

Becky went first, insisting she wasn't as tired as everyone else, as all she'd done at the warehouse was boss us all around and not do any heavy lifting. The pace of loading picked up as the fresh volunteers took over. When the last slab of cartridges was handed to me, we decided that we'd loaded enough onto the trailer and started loading one of the lorries. There were very few zombies in sight now, and as soon as one was in range it was felled by one or our snipers, so a few more of us left their guard positions to help in the final push. We carried on working.

I was standing inside the shop, passing items along the chain, when I heard the unmistakable sound of glass breaking, followed seconds later by a loud smash as something hit the pavement. Remembering the zombie in the window, I opened my mouth to scream a warning, but before a sound came out, two heavy thuds sounded outside, followed closely by yells of shock and panic from our party. Everyone in the shop dropped what they were carrying instantly and ran outside.

Marc had been standing in line, passing along whatever was handed to him when the glass broke. He cursed and shouted in pain as a falling piece of broken glass sliced deeply into his cheek. Earlier, he'd removed his helmet and coif when he was working hard, claiming it was making him too hot and if he needed to go and fight them, he could have them back on in seconds.

Holding a hand to his cheek, trying to stem the flow of blood, he'd been flattened by the dead weight of two bodies falling on him. Those around him stood shocked for the smallest of moments before dropping what they were carrying and rushing to his aid. Two writhing and snarling bodies covered him, their arms and legs kicking and grabbing as they tried to feast on the meal that fate had led them to land upon.

Knives and axes were pulled from belts as those around him attacked the zombies with hurried but practised efficiency and in seconds, the two limp bodies were dragged to one side. Marc lay curled on the floor holding his hands against his chest, bellowing in pain.

Ian reached to help him, but he shouted, "Don't! I think fuckers have bitten me!"

All around him, eyes closed in anguish, swearing and shouts of anger rang out as we gathered beside his prone form. Still holding his hand against himself, he pushed himself upright and sat on the ground, all eyes on him. Gingerly, he raised his hand to his face and stared at the wound. His wrist had a deep bite mark in it and was pouring with blood.

"Ah, fuck it," was all he said.

I was knocked aside as Jamie pushed past me and kicked him back to the floor. As he lay there stunned, Jamie swung his axe at his outstretched arm and severed it at the elbow. We all stood around, shocked at what he'd just done. Fresh blood was spurting from the stump of Marc's arm as Jamie threw his axe aside and screamed at the top of his voice.

"Get me a first aid kit!"

That galvanised some into action. Captain Hammond pushed past others while reaching into a pouch in his pack. He pulled out an aid kit and ripped it open as he fell to his knees beside Marc, who was lying in shocked stillness, staring at the stump that had once been his arm. With practised efficiency, Steve tied a tourniquet tightly around his upper arm and wrapped the bleeding stump with a bandage which immediately became soaked red with the blood that still poured from the wound.

My face white with shock at the events of the last minute, I stood numbly staring at Marc for a few more seconds until the captain shouted the command, "Let's get out of here right now! Help me get Marc onto the trailer."

Not knowing who was doing what, we milled around for a few more confused seconds before order was restored. A few of us carried Marc back onto the trailer gasping in pain and in shock. We laid him gently on the floor while others retrieved the few items that had been dropped when the zombies fell from the window, and threw them onto the nearest vehicles and scrambled onboard.

"Shawn. Lead the way," commanded the captain as keys were turned and one by one, engines fired up. A bit more disorderly this time, the convoy jolted forward and with engines roaring, we threw any caution to the wind and sped back to the castle.

All of us in the trailer only had thoughts for Marc and most of us crouched beside his prone figure, trying to cushion him as best we could from Shawn's wild ride as he pushed the tractor to its top speed.

He was pale faced and lying numb with shock. Tears streamed down his face and his mouth silently uttered curses as waves of pain washed over him and he gradually fell unconscious.

We didn't know what to say to him. Was he infected? Or had Jamie's crazy actions saved his life, stopping any infected blood spreading through his body when he hacked off his arm?

Captain Hammond's calm voice issued instructions as we drove. He told Shawn that they would pull ahead of us as we reached the castle so they could open the gates to allow him to drive straight through and get to the castle as quickly as possible. He would radio the ones in the castle and get them ready to open the barbican gates the second we were inside the castle grounds.

Grim faces full of concern exchanged silent looks as we comforted Marc the best we could. I was only aware we had arrived at the castle when we raced through the dim light of the barbican.

The tractor's racing engine echoed off the stone walls, making me look up. The increased noise roused Marc and he shouted heartbreakingly before slumping back into a semi state of unconsciousness, "I'm dead already. Don't let me turn, just kill me now so I can be with my wife and son again."

I put my hand on the hilt of the knife on my belt, but Becky saw me and shook her head.

"Don't, Tom. We know it takes ten minutes or so to turn after a bite. If he doesn't start showing symptoms soon, he may be clean. I think we should keep him in the trailer until we know. If we shut the door, sealing us in, a few of us can stay to keep him as comfortable as possible, we should know soon enough." We were still fifty-two, but for how much longer?

CHAPTER THIRTEEN

As soon as the vehicles stopped in the courtyard, everyone else dismounted and rushed to the trailer to check on Marc's condition. Those who had remained behind rushed forward too, but the news from the captain's urgent radio call hadn't spread to them all yet. Although, upon seeing how those who had returned were acting, they knew something had gone wrong. They were soon told.

Captain Hammond pushed through the crowd gathering around the trailer and jumped in as soon as the door was opened. Scrambling over the piled-up supplies that filled the bed of the trailer, he crouched beside Marc and inspected the blood-soaked bandages he had hastily wrapped around the shortened stump of his arm.

"I need more bandages," he shouted to no one in particular, as he carefully raised his arm and began removing them.

He looked up at me. "Does anyone have better medical training than I do around here?"

"I don't think so," I replied, "but we don't know if he's infected or not yet. It's only taken ten minutes or so for those who've been bitten to turn so far and he must be nearing that time now."

The captain jerked back slightly at the realisation dawned on him that he could be kneeling next to something that might start to bite him

Seeing this, I hastily added, "Don't worry, I've seen it happen and we'll get warning if he's going to turn. I think it's best, though, that until we know chopping his arm off has worked, we should shut the door on the trailer and isolate him from the others. If it's going to happen it shouldn't be long now."

He thought for a moment and nodded. "Okay, let's do that. But I need to try and stop the bleeding, or he won't make it anyway. The problem is that we're all trained in battlefield trauma, but that's only to keep them alive until they get to the medics. Marc needs more help than we can give him if he's going to make it; if he doesn't turn first, that is," he added with a grim smile.

He looked around at the ones still in the trailer. "Okay, folks. Can you all get out please and shut the door on us? Tom and I can take it from here until we know otherwise."

He raised his voice, "Sergeant Gallon. Where are you?"

His sergeant responded immediately from near the rear door, his Geordie accent sounding cheerful and reassuring.

"Yes Boss? Right behind ya."

"Get me every aid kit you can gather and then raise the fleet on the radio and get their surgeon on. We need to know what to do if by some miracle he doesn't turn."

With a, "Right you are, Boss," I heard him shouting orders as he ran to do his officer's bidding. It didn't take him long to gather and pass me an armful of packages, which I threw down next to the captain and then he closed the door on the trailer, sealing the two of us in. Glancing at my watch, I tried to work out how long

107

it had been since he had been bitten. It had to be over twenty minutes. Marc lay pale faced and still, a sheen of sweat across his face. He wasn't displaying any of the signs we'd seen before when we watched Louise's sister turn, all those days ago on Bodmin moor, and my hopes rose.

"Captain, what can I do?" I asked as I crouched down next to him.

"Just keep opening those packs, please. The tourniquet doesn't seem to be stemming the flow of blood much, so all I can do is keep changing bandages." He looked at me. "And for God's sake, can you call me Steve, please?"

We worked furiously on Marc for the next thirty minutes or so. By applying more pressure and changing the bandages, we managed to slow his blood loss to a level that Steve told me was acceptable. The problem was, we knew none of us had the expertise to give him a transfusion, or if we did, even what blood type Marc was. He'd lost a lot of blood, but had he lost enough to cause him more harm? That was a question none of us was qualified to answer.

Marc remained unconscious throughout and only groaned in pain as we changed his bandages. I knew that was a good sign because, if he could feel pain, then at least he was still human. Looking at my watch, I decided that he would surely have turned by now if he was going to. Talking it over with Steve, we both decided that it was probably safe to get him into the castle now. We would still keep a close eye on him in case he showed signs, but as we would continually be caring for him, it would just be something that those looking after him would need to watch out for.

We called from the trailer to those we knew were waiting close by to open it up and help get him inside. Using a board they'd already prepared, we carefully lifted him onto it and many willing hands gently carried him to the great hall.

The moment Steve and I stepped away from him, Becky and Sergeant Gallon bustled over to us. Becky was holding a notepad.

"Tom," she began, and I could tell from her manner that she was in business mode. "I've just had a long conversation with the ship's surgeon. He's told us what we need to do and what supplies we need to get." She looked at Steve. "We need to find a chemist or doctor's surgery, probably both if one doesn't have what we need." There's a chemist on the High Street, I remember seeing it as we passed it earlier, so if I give you the list, you need to get there right now."

She paused and looked concerned.

"The surgeon recommends cauterising the wound if we can't stop the bleeding."

I looked at her, my face displaying my lack of understanding. She raised her eyebrows to me in a look I knew all too well.

"Tom! We have to heat something red hot and seal the wound," she explained with an irritated tone. "Then he'll probably need a blood transfusion and a course of antibiotics to keep infection away. If he survives all that, then time and care will be the best recovery method."

I nodded soberly at the thought of what we needed to do.

"The chemist may have what we need to do transfusions. It should also have simple blood testing kits so we can find out whose blood is compatible." She handed Steve the list. "Can you get on it right away, please? The surgeon's waiting for me to report back on his condition."

Grabbing the list with a, "Yes, Ma'am," he turned and indicated for the four sergeants, Willie included, to accompany him so they could get on with planning the next mission.

Jamie rushed up to me as soon as he saw I was clear. "How is he?" he asked, his face full of anguish and concern. "I...I just reacted," he stammered, "D...did I do the right thing?" I looked at my hands covered in blood and slowly nodded my head.

"Yes. You absolutely did the right thing. It was bloody crazy to watch, but he hasn't turned yet. If he survives the blood loss and shock and hopefully avoids infection, Becky says she thinks he should live." Relief washed over him and his shoulders slumped as the tension and worry left him.

"What the hell made you act so quickly?" I asked. "I mean, we were all standing there like lemons and you barge forward like a mad axeman, kick him to the floor and chop his fucking arm off. How did you know what to do?"

He looked at me with a mystified expression as he thought of an answer.

"I haven't got a clue, really. I think I saw it in a movie somewhere. You know, that one with Brad Pitt. That soldier woman he was with got bitten by a zombie and he chopped her hand off to save her life. It just came to me and I knew there was no time to waste. If I did nothing, he was dead anyway, so I just did it without thinking, really."

I slapped his mail-clad back. "Brilliant, mate. I know Woody joked a few days ago that we needed to start watching zombie films and TV shows as a training guide and I think he's probably right. They'll have a whole load of stuff in them we haven't thought of or come across yet." I chuckled quietly. "I think we need to plan a visit to somewhere that sells DVDs soon and keep an eye out for a big television and DVD player."

I looked at the group of soldiers still deep in discussion in a corner of the large room. "Anyway," I continued, "let's leave that for another day because we need to go out again and get the medical supplies that Marc needs. Shall we go and see what we can do to help?"

Before any vehicle could leave, we first needed to empty them of the supplies we'd gathered, otherwise the mass of boxes and packages that littered the beds of them would make an unstable platform from which to battle zombies. Steve only wanted to take the tractor and armoured car on the mission to the chemist. Between them, they could take enough people to provide a strong fighting force and both vehicles had the power, strength and armour to smash through anything they came across.

Every available person who was not on guard or tending to Marc gathered in the courtyard and began unloading. There was no time to do a neat job and soon a massed, jumbled mountain of food, ammunition, weapons and a myriad other items we had gathered, piled up on the grass. The moment the last box had been unloaded, those chosen to go on the mission boarded the vehicles and sped out through the barbican as soon as the gates were opened, and the portcullis raised.

Not picked to go, I watched the small convoy roar out of the castle, the urgency of the moment not lost on the drivers, who were pushing the vehicles as fast as they could go.

111

Looking at the untidy mountain of goods, I gave a tired shrug and said to the group of bystanders around me, "Shall we start to make sense of this lot?"

Keeping the volume up on our radios so we could keep track of any progress, we began organising and stacking the goods into a semblance of order. Both army lorries, the crane lorry and Woody's Defender still stood where we'd left them earlier, all fully loaded with the rest of what we'd gathered. It represented a huge quantity of supplies and would probably take days to properly sort, catalogue and store in the right place. But doing what we were doing took our minds off our situation and stopped us dwelling on what had happened today.

None too distant gunfire caused us to pause and stare at each other. Some of us were once again out there facing danger, this time on a mission to get the supplies needed to save the life of another of our group. We had to trust they would keep themselves safe. As Steve had told those going on the mission, there was no time for subtlety on this one. Firepower, speed and maximum aggression was what was required to ensure its success and by the sound of the firing we could hear, that was what they were doing.

Eventually, we got a call through the radio of, "On way back. We've got what we need." That was all we needed to hear to stop what we were doing and gather, ready to help them when they arrived.

The tractor, driven by Shawn and closely followed by the armoured car, raced through the barbican and skidded to a stop, both vehicles cutting a long furrow in the grass of the courtyard as their wheels locked.

Eddy swung the back door of the trailer open and Chet, not waiting for the ramp to be lowered, jumped down and raced inside, carrying two full bags. When I'd helped lower the portcullis and outer and inner gates, I too went into the Great Hall to see what help I could offer.

Marc had been moved to the dining room, where we had the radio set up, and was lying on a camp bed surrounded by concerned people. His pallor had changed to a deathly grey colour and he did not look in good shape. Becky and Steve were sorting through the bags Chet had brought inside and were forming small piles of items.

I could overhear Becky as she talked to Steve. She'd been in communication with the surgeon when she could see Marc's condition deteriorating. What he needed was an immediate blood transfusion to replace all that he had lost. The advice given was that he needed to be stabilised before they attempted to cauterise the wound, otherwise the shock of the procedure could kill him.

I knew I was an O blood type, which from my limited medical knowledge, meant my blood was suitable for all blood types.

"Becky," I called to get her attention, "I'm an O blood type, remember. Doesn't that mean I can give blood to anyone?"

She snapped back, too preoccupied to even look up at me or have the time for pleasantries.

"Yes. Now sit down and you'll be the first I'll get blood from." She then called out to the room, "Can someone go around and ask if people know what blood type they are. Once I can test Marc's, I'll let them know if they're needed."

Ten minutes later, Becky finished another call to the surgeon, who seemed to be permanently on hand via the radio to offer whatever assistance and advice he could. I sat in a chair with my arm held out as Becky tied a strap around it. When the vein started to show, she held a needle ready with a valve on it.

I could see her hands shaking and the look of intense concentration on her face as she prepared herself.

"It's okay, darling," I said calmly. "You can do this. Now take a deep breath and take a moment to calm down. The way your hands are shaking, you'll turn me into a pincushion before you find my vein."

My poor attempt at humour did calm her down, though, and on the second attempt and with a few yelps of pain from me, she'd inserted the needle deep into my vein. Reaching for a tube with a bag at the end of it, she attached it to the valve and when she turned it, to a look of surprised triumph on her face, my blood started flowing down the tube and into the bag. Bob, also an O blood type, sat next to me with his sleeve rolled up and ready.

Steve had managed to insert a needle into a vein in Marc's arm, albeit with some difficulty, and as soon as the bag attached to me was full, he moved it over to Marc, and with Charles the vicar holding the bag in the air, he fixed it to the needle. We all sighed with relief as we saw the blood flowing down the tube and into Marc. It is not a quick process to transfuse blood, but eventually and after more donations from volunteers with the right blood match, Marc's pallor had faded and colour was returning to his face.

After confirmation from the surgeon about which of the many vials from the chemist was the right one to use, Becky used a hypodermic syringe to pump Marc full of painkillers and antibiotics.

The bad news was that as Marc received more blood, his wound began bleeding again, soaking the bandages that were tightly bound around his stump. We were going to have to cauterise the wound.

Becky once again consulted with the Surgeon about how to do it. Basically, what we needed to do was to heat up something and press it against the wound. The main thing was not to have the item too hot and only press it briefly against the wound, so not to damage any living flesh around it.

Insisting she wanted to perform the procedure, she asked someone to bring her one of the camping stoves and for one of us to find a suitable utensil or tool.

A short time later and with a few of us standing ready to hold Marc still, she held over the flame of the stove an old metal smoothing iron we'd found on display in one of the rooms, and heated it up. The second she nodded to us to get ready, we held his body down and she raised the iron shimmering with heat, and pressed it against the exposed blood-soaked stump of his arm that Steve held firmly with both hands.

The wound sizzled, filling our nostrils with the gag-inducing smell of burning flesh. Marc, still unconscious, writhed and bucked against the intense pain his brain must have been registering. Twice more she heated up the iron and pressed it against the wound, and each time Marc's movements became less frenetic as his body shut down, protecting him from further agony. Eventually, after studying the arm, she let the iron drop to the floor and stood back, satisfied she had done enough to stop the bleeding. Steve then coated the stump with an antiseptic ointment and wrapped it tightly in fresh layers of clean bandages.

Becky stood silently, staring at Marc's unconscious body. The emotion of what she had just had to do etched on her face, she said quietly, "I think we've done all we can do. Time is the only thing we can give him now."

Seeing the look on her face and knowing what she needed, I approached her and taking hold of her hand, led her outside, away from the cloying smell of burnt flesh and into the fresh air.

Understanding that she needed to be away from people, I guided her across the grass of the courtyard away from the main building, before enveloping her in a hug. "You did a fantastic job, my love. Well done, darling," I whispered in her ear. "I don't think anyone could have done a better job."

Resting her head against my chest tiredly, she replied, "I was shitting myself, to be fair. I was treating him from the start and it just didn't seem fair to take a step back and get someone else to take over. But the smell of the iron against his flesh! It took all I had not to drop it and run away." As the adrenaline drained from her system, she began crying and I hugged her tighter. Saying nothing, I stood hugging her, just giving her the time to let it all out.

Many long minutes later, she slowly began to recover. I still kept hugging her until she gently pushed me away, kissed me and said, "Thank you, I needed that. Now let's go back and see how he's doing."

We were still fifty-two and two dogs.

CHAPTER FOURTEEN

Marc was still unconscious. Even though he still looked deathly pale, I could see some colour had returned to his face, which I took to be a good sign.

He was surrounded by a team of carers who were keeping him under constant observation, so there was little that Becky or I could do to help without getting in the way. Gratefully taking two mugs of tea that were handed to me and passing one to Becky, we joined the throng of concerned, chatting adults and children who were gathering in the Great Hall.

When Steve saw Becky, he walked over and thanked her for everything she had done. "The surgeon is very impressed with how you handled the situation, Becky," he said with a smile. "You've no doubt saved his life."

Becky looked sad again. "But he has to live with half an arm now. His last words were begging for us to kill him so he could rejoin his wife and son. I think when he wakes up and begins to comprehend what's happened to him and how his life will change because of this, we might have to work hard to enable him to see the positives and not just the negatives of his future."

Steve nodded soberly. "I know. I've spent time with soldiers who've suffered many life-altering injuries and you're right. We'll have to make him understand that being alive is better than the alternative and that he can still be a valuable member of our community. He may not be able to wield his pike anymore, but he can still contribute to our survival in some way." He looked around the room. "There aren't many of us left and we're going to need every one of us if we're going to get through this."

Changing the subject, I glanced at my watch. "Talking about being useful, we've still got a few hours of daylight left and a mountain of stuff to sort through. Shouldn't we get on with sorting it?"

Steve nodded. "Just as you walked in, the sergeants were thinking along the same lines as well. There's no point us all mooching about brooding and a bit of manual work will help take everyone's mind off what's happened."

At the thought of doing something useful, he perked up and slapped me on the back, saying, "Shall we get on with it then!"

Watched over by the sentries patrolling the walls, everyone else who wasn't involved with caring for Marc or Sarah began the monumental task of sorting through everything we'd scavenged today. Rooms had already been designated as either food storage, sundry storage or as an armoury. First, we cleared the pile of hastily unloaded goods that we had thrown from the vehicles needed to go and get Marc's urgent medical supplies. All that was sorted and stacked in the relevant rooms under the guidance of a few who were cataloguing what we'd collected. The other vehicles were then backed up one at a time to the main doors and unloaded, until exhaustion took us over. And the need to eat the deliciously smelling food that was drifting from the kitchen made us call it a day.

***

Later that evening, we sat in the great hall by the flickering light of a few candles and lanterns. Marc, under the guidance of the surgeon, was being sedated and had not regained consciousness yet. After considering the reports of his temperature and vital signs, the doctor informed us that he was doing as well as could be expected. Marc now lay on a bed we had set up in the dining room and was being watched over by a rotating list of volunteer nurses, of whom Jamie was the most ardent.

Steve, who had been on the radio to the admiral, joined us after helping himself to a glass of whisky from a bottle that never seemed far from Willie. He updated us on the day's progress made by the fleet sheltering in the Solent.

"They're still waiting for two more Royal Navy ships to arrive and then every known asset they have will be there." He chuckled. "Apparently, the Solent is getting a bit crowded and looking like a fleet review with all the shipping gathering and small crafts trying to keep out of their way." He looked at the questioning faces staring at him. "Oh, Sorry. You know a fleet review? Like in the old days when Navies gathered all their ships together in a bit of a 'don't fuck with us' show of strength. But I imagine the mass of ships and small boats filling it is a bit more disorderly than the precisely lined-up rows of huge, great battleships I remember from photos of the old days.

"Anyway, I digress," he admonished himself and continued. "They're busy cataloguing all the supplies that are available from the manifests of the container and cargo ships that have also dropped anchor around them. A lot of it is useless junk and they're coming up with a plan to use those containers. If they can gain a foothold on the right dock and offload them using dockside cranes to form a barricade, they're hoping to be able to keep the zombies away so they can gain access to shore-based fuel reserves." He paused again. "Anyway, they're bandying around a lot of theories and ideas and not got up to much yet. Apart from sending helicopters, that is, now they have them, and patrols to search for any safe anchorages and signs of survivors along the south coast."

Pausing to sip from his whisky, he savoured it for a few seconds before continuing. "The helicopters are making the task a lot easier. The Scilly Isles are still looking the favourite place to head to, and following a helicopter overflight today, they're dispatching a few patrol craft to investigate further."

I interrupted him when a thought came into my head.

"Is there anything they want us to do here or are we just to make this place as secure as possible, hunker down and wait to see what happens?" Smiling humourlessly, I added, "To be fair, after today, I'm all for doing that."

Steve smiled along with everyone else at my attempt at levity. "They haven't asked anything of us. They know what we've achieved, but also know what we've been through and what a hell of a day we've just had.

I think they realise they don't need to worry about us for the moment and as we're so are far away from any area they're currently looking at, there's no need for us to do anything." He paused to sip at his drink again. "It'll most likely change when they turn their thoughts to the mainland. So yes, Tom, I think the best thing for us to do is to hunker down and secure our position."

He looked around at all of us.

"But I have a feeling that when the time is right, this place will become a springboard for future operations. Even though we've got enough food, weapons and other supplies for our own needs for probably quite some time, I think that we also have an obligation to gather as much as we can for others in the future. As long as we can do it without exposing ourselves to an unnecessary level of risk, that is."

He looked serious as he continued. "I made a promise to myself that I would do my utmost never to lose any more men under my command." He held his hands up and glanced at Maud. "And I know you're not under my command, as we all know who really is in charge around here." He waited for the chuckles to subside as Maud turned red. Willie put his arm around her and gave her a hug and a quick peck on the cheek. "When we go beyond our walls again, as you all know we must, then we take no risks. Not even the smallest one because as today has proved, you never know when shit will happen."

Most nodded in agreement or sat silently thinking about what he had said and the dangers that lay just beyond the walls of our castle and what the future would hold.

Chris broke the silence. "All the talk about helicopters and reconnaissance has got me thinking. Is there an airfield around here?"

"Why?" I asked, puzzled at the change of direction in the conversation.

"Well," he answered, "driving around is all we've done so far. Yes, our vehicles keep us safe, but we are limited to how far we can go and how long we can be out there before we push our luck too far. We know we can get as much food as we need, or indeed for anyone else who arrives, by just taking food lorries from the roads and motorways close around here. And that's not counting what we can get from warehouses and supermarkets. I'm also sure a few more trips to any gun shops in the area will give us enough bullets to last a long time. But if we're asked to go further afield, then the risk will increase proportionately." He stopped as if unsure of what he was about to say next. "How about if we could go by air?"

Everyone looked at him in silence.

"Chris, are you trying to tell us you can fly a plane?" I eventually stammered in reply, not quite sure if that was what he was implying.

He shrugged, "Well, not exactly legally. I *was* learning to fly and was very close to getting my licence when we found out Nicky was pregnant." He took her hand, smiling at her. "I put it on hold once I suddenly had far more important things to spend my money on. But given the right weather conditions, I can take off and land and navigate myself around reasonably confidently, I suppose. It's not that difficult, really, you just have to remember procedures and stuff. And on a good day, navigation is relatively easy, even without sat nav, because you can pretty much fly from town to town or landmark to landmark."

I sat back, thinking about what he had just said.

Steve spoke up, "Chris, what planes can you fly and what range do they have?"

Chris thought for a moment. "It does depend on wind speed, its direction and a host of other factors, but the plane I flew, a

Piper Warrior, could fly for about four hours or about five hundred miles, I think, from memory."

"So," Steve replied. "You're telling me we can reach pretty much anywhere in the UK?"

"Well, not exactly. Without refuelling, you have to half that as you need to get back as well and allow a margin of error," he answered with raised eyebrows, not wanting to point out his error in calculation. "But I reckon we could go anywhere within a two-hundred-mile radius of an airfield and we wouldn't have to worry about skirting controlled airspace or overflying cities, so we could fly in straight lines."

I started laughing. "How old are you, Chris?"

"Thirty. Why?" he replied.

"Because, when I was about thirty I did exactly the same. It can't even be called a mid-life crisis, because that's far too young," I said grinning. "And you know what? I was just about to qualify when Becky fell pregnant with Stanley, so I gave it up, too. Bloody coincidence or what!" I lowered my voice to a whisper. "Do you think it's a heinous plan by all wives to spoil a man's fun and stop his dreams of becoming Maverick from Top Gun?"

"Tom," Becky retorted. "No! It shows that at some time in your lives, men have to grow up and stop wasting money on stupid hobbies. Shame that you missed the bit about growing up. And can I point out that I never stopped you from flying again? You just found a new hobby to waste your money on, that's all, and forgot all about being Duck or whoever his sidekick was."

At this point, all the men immediately spoke up to remind her that nobody wants to be Goose; he dies.

Shaking her head in disbelief, she looked at the women and said, "Case proved. At least we can fight, ladies, because if we had to rely on these *boys* to protect us, I do not know what we would do!"

Once the room had stopped laughing, the conversation continued.

"Can anyone else fly a plane?" Steve asked. When he looked at the room full of shaking heads and negative responses, he looked at Chris and me and stated, "Well you are now our air force. All we need to do is get you a plane."

"Ah, come on," I complained. "It's been over ten years; I've forgotten it all by now. You can't be serious."

Steve held up his hands to stop any further comments from me. "I was being semi-serious, I suppose, but if you don't think you can do it, then don't worry about it."

The conversation moved on and we all began discussing what jobs or tasks would be prioritised tomorrow. After today's events, there wasn't much enthusiasm for leaving the castle, so it was universally agreed that for the next few days at least, we would concentrate on making our new home safer and more comfortable. We had more than enough food, weapons and ammunition to last us for the foreseeable future. Our own foreseeable future, that was. But we knew we'd need to go on gathering stuff, because there was no limit to what supplies we needed to store. These supplies, whatever they might be, would after all be not only for us, but for any more survivors we came across.

When tiredness and the knowledge I was on guard rota in a

few hours forced me to turn in, I still lay awake for a while. What Steve had said about an air force kept running through my mind. Could I still do it?

With Marc under constant care, fifty-two people and two dogs spent another night behind the walls of the castle.

CHAPTER FIFTEEN

Marc regained consciousness the next morning. The painkillers and sedatives he was being administered kept him in a semi-lucid state to try to give him the rest and time to recuperate which he desperately needed.

His emotional state though, was something that had us all worried. His opiate-filled mind raged from disbelief that he was alive, to anger that he *was* and that he'd lost most of an arm. His last conscious thought was that he was going to die and so be reunited with his wife and son and now he felt guilty that he had let them down and couldn't even fulfil what he thought was his dying wish.

His carers kept a close eye on him and constantly tried to re-assure him, but they knew that time was what he needed most; that, and helping him to understand and come to terms with what the future would hold for him.

Regular contact was maintained with the fleet, not only with the surgeon who was confident that the patient would make a full recovery, but with the admiral or one of his staff who kept them updated on the progress they were making.

The news was encouraging. A strong force had landed by hel-icopter and had secured one of the smaller, usually uninhabited islands of the Scilly Isles, where they'd killed the few zombies who, by some hand of fate, had found themselves marooned there. It wasn't large enough and had no infrastructure to support a large population, but it was a start and the marines and engineers who had accompanied the initial force were busy building a Forward Operating Base that would function as a helicopter refuelling and rearming site and also a safe haven, if the mission hit problems when the main operation began. The five largest and inhabited islands were still populated by thousands of zombies, but now they had a safe foothold on the islands, they could begin the operation to clear them. Some of the hundreds of civilian boats that had gathered around the fleet were being drafted in to help with the plan. There was a shortage of landing craft and the smaller private boats, with their shallow draft would make suitable enough improvised vessels. The similarities to Dunkirk, where small boat owners answered the call and helped rescue the hundreds of thousands of British and Allied soldiers trapped on the beaches was obvious. It was of course mentioned with pride by both the Royal Navy personnel and us, comparing it to how the remnants of the country's population were pulling together with one goal in mind: the survival and continuation of the human race.

All the owners whose boats were chosen had volunteered to command their craft, leaving more trained fighting people available for the mission. A frenetic few days of mission planning, personnel and equipment transfer would be needed until they were ready to depart.

Their strategists, though, were finding planning how to clear the islands problematic. None of them had any real idea of the capabilities required and difficulties involved with fighting the undead. We were the only ones who had real experience fighting the zombies and Steve was asked by the admiral to use our collective experience to come up with a battle plan to aid the men and women he was sending in to fight what to them would be an unknown enemy.

Calling an all-community meeting, Steve asked us to help him. We reviewed the tactics we'd developed as our experience and the number of people had increased, and also how it had changed our approach as we'd assimilated new weapons, skills and experience into our group. The knights had been a game changer for us, allowing us to go on the offensive against large numbers of them, without having to rely on expending large quantities of ammunition.

Information sent to us informed us that the population of the Scilly Isles was approximately two and a half thousand but, in the summer, that would increase by many more thousands as tourists flocked to the archipelago.

Now that one of the smaller islands had been secured, the initial plan they were working on was to use that as a base and to clear the islands one by one, using smaller, mainly civilian boats to ferry the sailors and marines about. It was how to do that with the least risk to everyone that they needed help on.

A few hours later, Steve had a long radio conversation with various Royal Navy personnel when he passed on the tactics and advice we had collectively drawn up.

When Steve had signed off, we continued with the plan to make the castle our home. The remaining supplies we'd gathered the day before were carried in from the courtyard, stored and catalogued. Furniture found in some of the myriad rooms the castle contained was moved to where it would be better utilised. Maud 'volunteered' people to help her in the many little tasks and jobs she was continually coming up with, each improvement making the castle more comfortable and homely. Willie began instructing some on how to manufacture bullets using the homeloading equipment we'd collected and soon had a small production line running, filling most of the empty ammunition cans we'd kept for that very purpose with a growing quantity of valuable ammunition. The knights, after seeking permission from Maud, searched the entire castle to sort through all the weapons and armour they deemed useful to us. They began to work on developing a training programme so everyone could practise using and gain experience with the weapon that suited them best. As our experience grew, they wanted us all to start drilling in groups to further develop the highly effective strategies they'd already formulated. Depending on the quantities of zombies facing us, it would give us the capability of fielding one larger group of armour-clad warriors or possibly smaller units who could work together to surround and destroy the threat.

As we practised with the unfamiliar weapons, our fitness, or lack of it, was plainly highlighted. Due to their comparative youth and the fact that they were more used to physical exertion, the original knights and the soldiers could cope with carrying the extra weight of armour and wielding a weapon better than the older 'civilians' amongst us. Simon, being a fitness instructor, was therefore tasked with improving the fitness and stamina of us all. Taking the role seriously, he conducted an individual survey of everyone in the group, assessing any medical or physical problems any of us had and was devising a tailored package for all of us which would include group fitness sessions.

While I wasn't a fan of gyms, or for that matter any exercise more than a game of tennis with my friends, or the occasional family cycle ride, I did know it made sense. It didn't stop me moaning and whinging about the proposed regime, though. I thought it was my duty to grumble, as any self-respecting slightly overweight, middle-aged man should, even though I knew there was not a lot I could do about it. Anyway, the way my legs and arms felt after only a few minutes of swinging the sword I'd chosen as my preferred weapon, it was obvious that my personal fitness needed improving.

A few zombies kept appearing at the second gate, so we searched for where they were getting in and repaired the fence, which had been damaged by a fallen tree.

Shawn and Jon began constructing shelters on the ramparts to protect the sentries from the elements. The sounds of sawing and of cordless power tools being used was a necessary evil, but we knew the shelters that were springing up around the ramparts would be a great improvement and make enduring sentry duty in inclement weather a more comfortable prospect.

In other words, everyone got on with the job of living there.

The next two days passed quickly as the bonds that already held us together were strengthened by working on one of the many tasks we came up with and completed together. We were becoming an extended family and not just a group of survivors.

CHAPTER SIXTEEN

Just off Hugh Town, St Mary's, The Scilly Isles

Marine Captain Digby stared through his binoculars at the nearby town; the largest in the islands. Smoke still drifted lazily away on the breeze from a few burnt-out buildings, but they did not occupy his attention. The thousands of shambling, slow moving figures that wandered everywhere did. They filled the once picturesque town, spilling out onto the harbour front and beaches that would normally, this time of year, be filled with tourists.

"These *are* the tourists," he thought bitterly to himself as the magnified vision picked out individuals in the throngs of undead. Some were still wearing their pyjamas, while some were dressed in shorts and T-shirts or even just swimming costumes. Evidence was everywhere of the speed with which the virus and the ensuing waves of zombies had engulfed a totally unaware and unprepared population. A pang of sadness washed over him. His own sister and her family were unaccounted for. He knew that they should have been on holiday in Cornwall, somewhere in their caravan when the outbreak began. Following the reports on the conditions on the mainland, he did not hold out much hope of them having survived. He swallowed the emotions that welled up inside him at the thought of his sister Anne, his brother-in-law Trevor and his nephew Eddie.

How old is Eddie? he thought angrily at the unfairness of it all. It was years since he'd seen him due to the long tours and postings he'd been on, his knowledge of him only updated by the regular social media updates his sister posted. He now regretted the times he could have visited but had chosen instead to just call his sister when he remembered to do so.

Hugh Town was where they were going to begin their campaign. It was the largest population centre on the island and apart from the airport, home to the only port capable of accepting larger boats and ships and therefore the only way to get to the mainland. When the outbreak began it would have been the obvious place for the panicking, terrified population to head to as they desperately tried to escape. The wreckage of many small boats and yachts littered the foreshore, testament to the many failed attempts by people either too inexperienced or possibly too ill to pilot their own, or a stolen craft in a last-ditch attempt to escape by boat to safety.

In charge of the marine detachment chosen for the initial assault, he looked at the men gathered beside him on the rail of the type twenty-three frigate he was aboard. All were lost in their own thoughts as they mentally prepared themselves for the battle to come. The battle that would begin their goal to free the British Isles from the tides of death that covered its lands. And on a more personal note for all of them, to avenge their own lost loved ones.

The battle plan was as unusual as it was simple. Following advice from a team of survivors who had fought across the country and were now safely behind the walls of Warwick Castle, they had planned the mission.

The Frigate would approach the only place with a deep enough channel to allow a vessel of its size to near the shore; the harbour. Holding position just off from the jetty, they would sound the ship's horn continuously. The noise, they were assured, would attract every undead on probably the whole island in their direction. All they should have to do next was simply to wait as they dumbly walked off the stone jetty and drown in the deep water. When no more appeared, then they would land and clear the island house by house, mopping up any last traces of them.

They all carried, in addition to their usual weapons, a melee weapon. The engineering sections on all the Navy's ships had been working nonstop producing these short handled attacking weapons from whatever materials they had available or could scavenge from non-essential parts from all the ships. These were attached to their webbing by holders just as cobbled together. The designs varied as much as the materials used to make them, but they were all made from a template based around a hatchet or a mace.

When the men and women were first issued with them and they practised wielding them, getting used to the weight and feel of the one they had chosen brought reality home to them. Attacking with a bayonet attached to your rifle was something they were all trained to do. Very few times in recent history, though, had soldiers had to resort to using them. It all seemed a bit old fashioned to them, reminiscent of British redcoats fighting on the fields of Europe against Napoleon, using single shot, slow to load muskets, and not relevant in the modern world. But now they all carried a weapon that they would soon be smashing into the head of what was once a living person so they could destroy its brain.

Once the Island of St Mary's was clear, they would then use the many small privately-owned boats that had accompanied them. More were still arriving, as they couldn't keep up the pace set by the frigate over open water. They would use these small boats to ferry them to the other islands, and if the tactics worked, use them again.

The ship's horn blaring made him jump. He looked around, embarrassed at being caught out by it, but smiled when he saw the expressions on those around him all showing a similar reaction.

"Okay, chaps," he called, "double check your own kit and that of the one by your side. Make sure you can't cram another bullet anywhere on you. We'll be going in soon."

The ship's horn continued to echo around the harbour and beyond. Captain Digby watched with professional interest as the previously aimlessly shambling zombies turned as one to the deafening blasts of the ship's horn and moved towards the ship.

The ones on the beach just turned and knowing the noise that had disturbed them came from the big grey object not far from them, took the most direct route and walked into the sea. Undeterred by the water that got deeper with every step, they continued wading until a wave knocked them over, leaving the watchers with what would have been in other circumstances a brief comedic scene of uncoordinated arms and legs flailing as they disappeared below the surface. Others just simply kept walking until they were completely submerged, small ripples on the surface following their progress for a short time until he presumed they'd drowned or were too deep to disturb the surface of the sea. He hoped for the former, but he still cast his eyes down to the sea, where in the clear water of the sheltered bay they were in, he could distinguish between the light and dark of either sand or seaweed beds on the ocean floor.

As he stared down, his mind could not help but conjure up the terrifying image of an army of the undead marching towards them along the seabed.

Others in the town, prevented from falling off the harbour wall by its railings, continued along the sea front until channelled along the jetty that reached out towards the ship.

Once Captain Digby had overcome his initial revulsion and more than a little fear at seeing zombies close up for the first time, he studied them intently. They acted, he had been informed in the many briefings he had attended when planning the mission, not unlike the traditional slow-moving, shambling zombies portrayed on many television shows and movies, and fortunately not like the fast-moving super zombies others portrayed them as.

They dumbly followed one another, moving together as one seething mass. When the leading ones neared the ship, they stretched out their arms, their fingers searching for the meal their remaining senses told them was contained in the ship holding position three yards from the sheer stone walls of the harbour's jetty. The gap between the jetty and the ship did not register in their simplified brains and without faltering, they just stepped off the edge and tumbled into the water below. Some sank immediately from sight into the dark shaded water, whereas others remained floating for a short time as air trapped in their clothes buoyed them up until slowly they, too, sank from sight.

The sailors and marines lining the rail alongside him initially cheered and whooped at the sight of so many comically tumbling into the water, scoring marks out of ten for a particularly skilful dive. Digby did consider ordering them to stop, but from the exaggerated cheers and cat calls coming from the servicemen and women, he soon realised that after many continual days of setbacks and bleak news, combined with personal worries about their own loved ones, they needed to let off steam. Also, seeing the zombies hopefully so easily led to their deaths would boost everyone's morale at a time when everyone needed it.

After five minutes, though, of watching hundreds of zombies fall like lemmings into the water, the watchers quietened down. More of them were still pouring onto the dock and the end of the shambling mass was not yet in sight. Even though they had proved easy to kill, the sheer numbers of them more than equalised any advantage people thought they had using weapons, manoeuvrability and tactics.

Moving away front the rail, Digby sat on a bollard and ran through the mission in his head. He could see no flaws in the plan they had devised. Once they'd landed, they would remain in one single group. Smaller squads within the group would detach to clear houses and buildings, but never be far from the protection of the main force. If large numbers of zombies were discovered, they would try to draw them out to an area where they could bring the biggest concentration of gunfire on them.

A Merlin helicopter would be flying reconnaissance overhead, keeping him informed of what was in the surrounding area.

Machine guns had been mounted on every suitable place on them, so if need be, they could provide close support for those on the ground If required, other helicopters that would be held in reserve on the small islet they'd already cleared could be called upon to assist. These were being deliberately held back to preserve them in optimal condition, should the mission go badly wrong and an emergency evacuation was required.

The kit each marine and sailor carried was cut to the minimum. They were only taking water and bullets, but they would all be carrying a large quantity of ammunition with them; a lot more than they usually carried on combat missions. If they expended this, the helicopter would also be able to resupply them by winching down loaded magazines in nets already loaded onto it.

He could find no flaws in the plan, although he reminded himself of the age-old adage that 'no plan survives first contact with the enemy'.

He was snapped from his thoughts by shouts and commands being issued. Standing up, he saw people pointing over the rail. Rushing forward to see what was happening, he was shocked to see the bodies were no longer splashing into the water but falling on the piled-up bodies that had built up enough to break the surface. As they landed on the ones beneath them, they tried to stand until hit by another falling on top of them.

More were still filling the jetty and it was not a stretch of the imagination to see that they could build up enough to enable those still coming to walk over the bodies of the ones below them and potentially reach the ship.

The horn on the ship stopped blaring and the loudspeaker warned everyone they were repositioning the ship. The ship's thrusters caused the water to boil at its bow and stern. Racing water washed over the piled-up bodies. As the ship began to move away, the powerful currents created underwater disturbed the bodies trapped below the surface, causing the sickening mass of stacked-up bodies to collapse in places. Bodies swirled in the eddies created, some still thrashing around, but some Digby noticed lay still and lifeless, proving the theory that they still needed to breathe to live and so would drown in water.

The captain of the ship skilfully brought the ship to a halt and held it in position another twenty metres from the jetty. This time he announced the horn would begin sounding again, most likely to warn people to put their mugs of tea down to save spilling it all over themselves when they jumped with the sudden blaring sound.

Digby watched with despair as the plan they had come up with to use the jetty to enter the town became impossible, as the remaining ones still kept walking straight off the edge to pile up in a macabre pile of writhing bodies. The ones that could move still crawled towards the ship over the ones piled up below them, their attempts ending in failure when they plunged off the edge and into the deep water of the harbour.

Digby looked at the beach. A few stragglers still walked into the water towards them, eventually disappearing under the surface, as all those before them had. The water's edge, though, was thick with the bodies of those washed back to shore by the incoming tide. They rolled slowly in the gentle surf that broke on the shore. Raising the binoculars that hung by a strap around his neck, he studied them. It was impossible to tell if they were alive or dead as the waves gently washed over them.

Some must surely be alive…mustn't they? he thought glumly. It looked as if the plan would have to change dramatically after their first contact with the enemy, he decided ruefully. The jetty was unapproachable now due to the piled-up bodies, and landing on the beach looked too risky as nobody would know if they were alive or dead until they stepped amongst them.

He looked around for the section leaders amongst the ones still lining the rail, muttering to himself as he noticed them standing in a group, probably already discussing the dangers that were evident to all of them of even trying to get to shore.

"Back to the drawing board it is, then!"

CHAPTER SEVENTEEN

Warwick Castle

Under guidance from the ship's surgeon, the quantity of sedatives marc was being administered was being reduced. Everyone was trying to be as positive as they could around him, but he even admitted to himself as well as to us that it would take him time to adjust to his new condition. He had joked, which proved he was trying to drag himself out from the deep state of unhappiness and depression he was in, saying that he was sorry if he had left them 'shorthanded' and if anyone asked him 'if he could lend them a hand', they'd better be a faster runner than he was.

After a few days pottering around the castle, I could tell that some people were getting restless. Walking across the courtyard, I looked up and saw Captain Hammond leaning on the ramparts looking over the grounds of the castle. I'd just finished helping Shawn and Jon rig up a water pipe from the river.

The castle would have employed a small army of maintenance staff responsible for the day-to-day repairs needed to keep the fabric of the historic and ancient building in good order. We had discovered the small yard and buildings they had used, hidden behind a gate when we'd searched the castle grounds. It had yielded a good supply of tools and other useful equipment, including some submersible water pumps which would most likely have been used if an area of the castle flooded for some reason.

Shawn, helped by me and a few others, joined a series of fire hoses together which, when the pump was plugged into the generator, delivered water from the river below. This water then passed through a series of cobbled together jerry-built filter systems to eventually fill thoroughly cleaned commercial waste bins to provide water for cooking, cleaning and flushing the toilets in the castle.

The system leaked and the filters were basic, but we knew through trial and error they could be improved over time. The water wasn't fit for drinking and we were still using bottled water from our supplies, and although we had enough to last for a few weeks, they would need to be replenished or an acceptable way invented to make the water potable. With nothing better to do, I climbed the steps that reached up to the ramparts and joined Steve as he leant on the wall staring at the grounds and the town beyond them.

"Everything okay?" I asked cheerily, still pleased from the work I'd just completed. "The water system seems to be working fine, so at least we'll be able to flush the toilets a bit more regularly now." Steve snapped himself out of his reverie and looked at me as my words sunk in, before replying somewhat distantly.

"Oh, yes. Good work." He looked over the walls again for a few moments before turning to me. "It's just that I think we've done all we can here, and I know there's a lot more still to do out there," he said as he waved his hand towards the world beyond our sanctuary. "It's just the 'what' part of to do I'm struggling with."

I smiled at him. "So, you want to go out there and be a hero again. Is that what you're trying to say?" I paused as I, too, looked outwards. "I think you're right. We've got over the shock of Marc and we know the mistakes we made that let that happen. The castle is as secure as it's going to be." I slapped him on his back. "Unless you can find us a few tanks, of course." I waited to continue, letting him laugh politely at my poor joke. "But I do know what you mean. I think we can start looking outwards again. There are still plenty of supplies to gather at that food warehouse and I know Shawn was saying we only have a few days' worth of petrol for the generators remaining. Why don't we raise it later after dinner? If we're thinking this way, I'm sure others must be too."

"Yes, good idea," he replied. "Let's do that. It's not just that warehouse, and gathering more supplies for ourselves, though. I'm not saying that's not an important job, but I've been thinking about how little we know about the rest of the country. There are still military and other officials trapped in bunkers and possibly other communities like us out there. At least, I hope to God there are. If we're going to take this country back, it can't just be the Navy and us few doing it, because there's no way that's going to be enough." He sighed and paused to lean heavily on the solid stone blocks of the ramparts. "I just think that once this place is not just impregnable, but has enough supplies to last for an extended period, then it's my duty to go out there to start doing what I can, no matter how small and insignificant it may be.

"I'm eager to hear how the Navy has fared in the Scilly isles. The plan and tactics we devised for them should hopefully make it as risk-free as possible, but as we know to our peril, nothing is risk free when we're dealing with those undead bastards." His voice turned sombre. "If they struggle against what should be a relatively small population on the islands, with all the resources and firepower they can bring to the party, then we will all have to rethink what to do next."

He barked a short laugh and reproaching himself for his moment's negativity, continued, "Ah, snap out of it, Steve! No point dwelling on what we don't know about yet. Come on, do you fancy a little sparring practice? I'm still trying to get used to the weight of the armour and after a few swings, my mace feels like a twenty-pound sledgehammer."

"Not just me, then," I quipped back with a grin. "I don't know how those boys do it. After five minutes I'm dripping with sweat, knackered and about to fall over, and if I do, there's no way I'll be able to get back up with all that weight on me. They can seem to keep doing it for hours. It does give you a lot of respect for medieval soldiers, though, and what they had to endure. I think they were a hell of a lot tougher than any of us."

"Yep, I agree," he replied as we both headed towards the stone steps to return to the courtyard. "I thought I was fit, but to fight with all that weight on, it's a whole other level. I think this fitness programme Simon's coming up with is going to do us all a world of good."

***

An hour later, the two of us were exhausted and fit to drop, but at the same time happy. The two of us and a few others who joined us when they saw what we were doing had gone through the drills we'd been taught by the more experienced knights. Facing an invisible enemy, we had practised with the pikes and forming shield walls, all the time learning how to move wearing armour and how to handle our chosen weapons more efficiently.

Chatting together, we all trooped into the Great Hall and began removing our armour. Looking up, I saw Becky walking into the room carrying a heavy box. Letting my armour drop to the stone floor with a loud clang, I went to help her. When I was two feet away from her, she took one look at my dishevelled, sweaty self and wrinkled her nose in disgust.

"Tom," she said, "I know washing is something we haven't been doing much of lately but look at the state of you." She looked at the rest of the men and women who had been on the practice field and raised her voice. "And if you all stink like this man in front of me, I think Maud will have something to say about it. Ladies," she said with a smile, "I know we've got more water to use now and I think Maud said she would heat some up for washing. If you want to go and help her, you can all have a nice hot wash."

She then looked at me and the men. "As for you lot!" She laughed when as one, the men all instinctively raised their arms and tried to smell their armpits. "You tough men can use the water outside in the bins."

"What, wash with cold water?" I exclaimed indignantly.

"Yes, if you want to come anywhere near me tonight," she replied haughtily and walked off to join the women, who were heading for the kitchen area.

Half an hour later, ten men who had washed using the cold water in the bins decided it would be a good idea to light the fire in the Great Hall's huge fireplace to try and stop shivering.

***

Willie emitted a belch as he scraped the last few morsels off his plate. Maud raised her eyebrows at what she considered a breach of etiquette at the dining table we had all crammed around. The table was huge, but there were so many of us around it, it reminded me of school dinners from my childhood, where too many of us sat on a bench and knocked elbows with our neighbour as we tried to eat the barely digestible food that the kitchen produced. The food this time, though, was excellent.

"Och, woman," he said gruffly, his eyes betraying his humour, "it's your fault for making such a fine meal. It was a sign of appreciation, that's all."

"Thank you, Willie," she replied coyly. She still showed embarrassment when anyone offered her praise, which we all did a lot as she worked tirelessly. Always bustling around, making sure 'her realm' as she had begun to call the cooking and living quarters, were maintained to her satisfaction. "But I didn't do it all by myself, you know. You should thank everyone that helped."

"I know others helped, my dear," he replied, trying to keep his expression serious. "But, you see, I like them and appreciate their efforts, but it's you I love, so I'm sure they'll excuse my rudeness at not including them."

We all cheered and banged the table at his gallantry, as Maud once again went bright red with a mixture of elation and embarrassment, saying in a voice that was barely audible above the noise we were all making, "Stop it, you big silly man."

When the room had quietened down, I stood up. "Come on, lads," I said, "let's get the washing up done and then we can all plan the next few days." Gathering up the dishes and plates, we soon had the table cleared, the dishes washed and stacked neatly in the kitchen. Then we went back to the others, including Marc, who had insisted that we help him from his bed so he could join us, and we all settled down in our favourite chairs around the still blazing fire.

Helping ourselves to a drink, everyone sat in companionable silence for a time, comforted and mesmerised by the dancing flames.

Steve stopped our daydreaming by coughing to get our attention and saying, "Right, folks, I think we have everything in the castle as good as it needs to be for now." He looked at Marc. "Marc, you're on the mend now, which is fantastic news. But we still need to gather more supplies and a whole host of other things which I know are still not ticked off the list."

Marc used his good hand and gently raised his arm that was still covered in bandages in the air. The room quietened down as we all realised he wanted to speak.

"I've had time to do a lot of thinking the past few days. Now that the sedatives have worn off and I'm not hallucinating anymore and seeing pink rabbits flying over the bed," he said with a smile, waiting for the chuckles to subside before continuing, his face now full of emotion. "I haven't thanked you all yet for what you've done for me. I know I said some horrible things and I apologise unreservedly for them, but I wasn't in my right mind. All I could think about was not being with my family and the promise I made to them over their graves that one day I would join them." Tears began to run down his face as the still raw memory of their tragic deaths hit him again.

"I know now I'm not ready to fulfil that promise. One day I will be, but for now I'll serve their legacy better by continuing and fighting on as best I can. I may not be able to wield a pike yet but when I am healed, maybe we can make a prosthetic or something that will enable me to.

Fighting may be out of the question for now, but soon I'll be able to use one hand to fire a pistol or swing an axe or sword.

Until then, you don't need two hands to keep guard." He paused and looked at us all as we sat in silence.

"I suppose what I'm trying to say is thank you and I do not intend to be a burden, but to keep helping in whatever way I can."

The room remained quiet until Jamie spoke up. He'd been the one who chopped his arm off in the aftermath of the brief fight with the zombies; saving his life in doing so. He'd made himself his primary carer ever since and had rarely been away from his bedside. Caring for all his needs and always trying to lift his spirits when he was in the depths of despair.

"Mate, you don't know how guilty I've felt. I've been filled with doubt about whether it was the right thing to do or not, and if we should have let you fulfil what was, as you thought at the time, your dying wish. Now, with what you've just said, I know it was the right thing to do." He stood and walked over to him and being careful to avoid his arm hugged him, saying as he did so, "Welcome back, mate."

Ian couldn't keep the conversation serious anymore and spoke up, "Oh no! Keep Jamie away from me in future. If one of us gets the tiniest of scratches on them, he's going to start swinging that axe of his around, thinking he's Florence Bloody Nightingale, out to save all out lives."

When the room had stopped laughing Steve carried on with the discussion he'd begun before Marc had interrupted him. "As I was saying, now we're back to full strength, I think we should start looking outwards again; not just for our own needs, but at the wider world around us.

This time, though, we won't complicate matters by trying to gather from more than one place. We go somewhere, grab what we can, get back and reorganise for the next trip. I think it'll be safer for all of us that way."

He held up a list he had pulled from his pocket as he was speaking.

"Tomorrow, I propose we start nice and easy and hop over the perimeter walls to raid and secure the houses that back on to it. We should be able to find a large enough television in one of those houses and as we've already discussed, if we can find some of those zombie films on DVD, then we can start some proper research.

All we've been doing so far is just making it up, we need some tips from the experts." He looked at the list again as he smiled at his own joke. "For the following day, I suggest we find fuel. Hopefully, it'll be a case of scouring the nearest motorway for a tanker to bring back. If we find a full one, it should keep us going for a long time. And then we can start to look at the rest of the list," he glanced at it again, "which is long, by the way. Does anyone have any comments or thoughts on that?"

He looked around the room. I knew from our conversation earlier what he was going to propose, so I'd been giving it some thought.

"You mentioned the wider world. Where do you suggest we start?"

"Good question, Tom," he replied. "As you know, there are forces trapped in bunkers in locations around the country." He looked at his watch. "I have our regular radio call scheduled with the fleet in ten minutes. I'll ask for the locations of them and see if any are within reach. Hopefully, they'll have an update on the operation on the Scilly Isles as well. As soon as they can get themselves and the civilians established there, the sooner they, too, will start to look outwards."

Since we'd had the conversation about flying and how Chris had been learning, as had I many years before, it had been rumbling away in the back of my mind. *Can I still do it? Will it be safe?* I kept asking myself. I'd gone through the memories of the flights I had done. Especially the solo flights you had to do before qualifying, and I'd come to the conclusion that as long as the plane was in good mechanical order and the weather made the visibility good enough, it was probably not a bad idea and I could do it. Before I opened my mouth, I silently went through any more pros and cons of the idea; not coming up with anything I hadn't already thought of, I made my decision and stood to get everyone's attention.

"Steve, remember the discussion about flying we had a few days ago? I've been mulling it over and I think that, despite my initial reservations, it might be possible." I looked at Chris, who had leant forward in his chair at the mention of flying. "If you agree, Chris, that is."

Chris nodded, "I'm up for it if you are."

Grinning at him, surprising myself as I felt my excitement building at the chance of being able to fly again, I replied, "As long as we get one thing straight first of all. I'm Maverick, though. You can be Ice Man!"

"There they go again," muttered Becky in mock disgust.

Steve stood up. "Thanks, guys," he said. "I'll report your decision to the fleet, I'm sure it will get their full support. Now if you would excuse me, I'll check in with them. Corporal Side, could you come with me and check the radio is good to go, please?"

We all sat in silence as Steve updated us on the failed attempt to land on and clear the largest of the islands.

"They're not considering it a failure, just a learning process. The tides and currents have now swept most of the beach clear. The jetty, unfortunately, because it's protected from the worst of those, is still not viable, so in the morning, they will attempt landing their forces directly onto the beach. They're confident they can do it; they'll just have to get a little wet, that's all."

CHAPTER EIGHTEEN

The Scilly Isles

Captain Digby sat on the inflated side of the large rib as it sped towards the rapidly approaching shore. Raising his voice over the noise of the boat's engine and the helicopter as it flew low overhead, its downwash buffeting them causing the calm seas around them to erupt in spray, he shouted to the men and women around him.

"Everyone, remember the drill. Stay calm and watch your backs." He turned his neck and looked towards the frigate, which looked huge in the confines of the bay. Following the lead boat he was in was a small armada of private craft, all carrying a complement of marines or sailors. More were lining up by the frigate, each one loading more to ferry ashore.

His boat was the lead element of the invasion force he was commanding. The initial task was to form a beachhead and protect it until they had a large enough force ashore to begin the operation. As predicted, the tide had swept most of the zombies away from the shore, but the bay was still thick with floating bodies, forcing the RIB to alter its course around them to avoid one fouling the propeller.

Throughout the remainder of yesterday and into the evening until the need for people to sleep forced it to be silenced, the Frigate had kept its horn blaring, drawing what they hoped was the rest of the island's undead population to the beach and harbour. The hope was that they would follow each other into the surf or off the edge of its walls, hopefully to die a second time in the waters of the bay. The plan seemed to have worked. As dawn had broken, Digby, along with what looked like most of the ship's complement, had eagerly lined the ship's rails to see the results. A few could be seen wandering through the town and along the beaches and quay, but they were fewer than they'd witnessed yesterday.

The mission was given the go ahead.

With a final rev of the engine, the RIB steered to a section of the beach where no zombies remained trapped in the rolling waves. It crashed through the low surf and hit the shelving sands of the beach, and as soon as the boat ground to a halt, Digby leapt from it and waded the final few yards through the knee-deep water to reach dry land.

"On me!" he screamed to those he could sense leaping into the surf behind him. Quickly they formed a semi-circle on the beach, all with their weapons trained outwards. The few zombies still on the beach already attracted by the sound of the boat's engine were shambling towards them.

Digby stared through the sights of his rifle at the nearest one before raising his head to assess the area around them. "Hold fire," he ordered. "Let them get closer. There's not many of them, so save ammo until you can be sure of a head shot."

The Marine beside him, his sergeant, fired his rifle and the head of a zombie fifty yards away burst apart and it crumpled to the sand.

"I'm sure," the man said grimly and shifted his aim, felling all the ones within a hundred yards one by one with a single shot to the head.

More than impressed by the display of marksmanship, Digby turned to him and chuckled, "Bloody hell, Sergeant. Can you leave some for the rest of us?"

The man deftly ejected his magazine and slapped home a new one and charged his rifle. "Sorry, Sir," he replied with a sad smile. "Those bastards, or…well, at least others like them, have probably killed my family and I needed to get that out my system." He paused and looked at those he'd just shot. "I'll follow your orders from now, Sir."

Digby looked at the bodies lying on the sand and then out to sea and slapped the man on the back. "Sergeant, you *did* follow my orders. Now, can we begin to increase our cordon? The other boats are just about to land." Then, as he thought of his own family, he added quietly, so that only his sergeant could hear, "Don't worry, Sergeant Austin, we've all lost loved ones whom we need to avenge. Just keep it together and don't go off doing something stupid on your own; I need you by my side." Grinning, he added, "Especially now I've seen you shoot like that."

His Sergeant looked at him. "Yes, Sir!" he replied and added, "I may angry, but I ain't stupid. No way I'm going Rambo on them. You can rely on me."

The more that landed, the bigger the beachhead they created, until all the marines and sailors were ashore. The loud crack of rifles firing continually rolled across the sand as more zombies kept appearing from the town, either individually or in small groups.

"Okay, received and understood," Digby said into his radio after listening to an update from the helicopter that was sweeping low over the town. He signalled to the lieutenants and sergeants to gather on his position.

"Okay, chaps," he began with as much cheer as he could muster, knowing they were about to face something they'd never trained for or even imagined they'd have to until a few days ago. "The chopper is reporting not many more sighted in the town, so we go as planned." He added more to reinforce it for himself as much as for those facing him. "Remember the briefing. Keep everyone together, the last thing we want is for us to get separated. When we enter a building, it will be just as important to watch our backs as well as whatever the hell might be going on inside.

You've all played the games, now let's go and do this for real."

Speech ended, he led the men and women to start the first operation to clear a town in the British Isles of the undead.

CHAPTER NINETEEN

"Who the heck needs a TV that size!" I asked as I stood in the lounge of one of the houses that backed onto the castle.

"We do!" came the reply from all around me.

I was on the team that had volunteered to search and secure the houses that bordered our new home. Using ladders to climb the walls or fences, we'd first studied each property carefully so we could see if they held any of their former owners, before entering the rear gardens. A few did, but working together as we were, they posed no threat to us as we smashed our weapons into their heads.

Once all the houses we were going to search had been declared safe and their frontages that opened onto the town of Warwick had been secured to make them resistant to any zombie attack, we began scavenging.

We were on the lookout for TVs and we knew every home would contain at least one, so we decided to leave the decision of which one to take until we'd checked them all.

We also knew every house would also contain some food, drinks and other useful items. After the initial search, during which we'd counted how many beds were in all the houses, we decided it would be worth dismantling them and taking them back with us. Most of us were still sleeping on air beds or camp beds and a soft mattress was something those of us not lucky enough to have one anymore longed for.

One property, a large one with a nice car on the drive at the front even had a gun safe. After a quick search, much to the amusement of the women, I found the keys to it hidden in the usual place; in the sock drawer of the former man of the house. The one thing we had plenty of was firearms, but as we all knew, enough would never be enough, so I emptied the gun safe of the lovely matching pair of shotguns it contained, along with a few hundred cartridges. Shane, on the mission with us, admired them and when he told me what they probably cost, we both decided so keep them separate from the others out of respect for their age and heritage.

Louise had overheard us excitedly admiring and discussing them and she brought us back on mission by saying in an exasperated tone, "So, with all the guns we already have, now you want to start a museum to display the pretty ones?" She laughed when she saw our faces as we tried to deny it. "Don't worry, boys, I'll keep your secret safe if it makes you happy."

As Shane put them into the gun slips hanging by the gun safe, I whispered to him, "Put 'em in your room. I'll have a look later." He winked at me and we got on with the job.

Although we'd all planned this to be a quick mission, it took most of the day to empty the houses of anything useful and then to dismantle and move all the beds and mattresses. They had to be carried one by one to the end of the gardens, lifted over the wall and loaded into the trailer.

When we got back, Shawn backed right up to the doors of the Great Hall and we unloaded everything. Later that evening, the castle more represented a furniture-building world champion-ship when we started to reassemble all the beds.

Once they'd helped with bed building, Jon and Shawn set about installing the huge seventy-inch television we'd removed from the wall of one of the houses. Using the brackets for it which we'd unbolted from the wall it was fixed to, after much discussion with Maud about where she would allow them to put it, they bolted it to the wall next to the fireplace in the Great Hall.

It looked incredibly out of place. A modern invention from the twentieth century fixed to the weapon- and tapestry-draped ancient walls of a historic building. But we needed it for a pur-pose. We'd found a DVD player and in a cupboard of one of the houses, we discovered to our delight a large collection of film and box sets, including a few zombie series and movies. The house we found them in had contained the former family, including their teenage children, which probably accounted for the wide variety of viewing material we had found.

My emotions were mixed about the television. I knew the op-portunity to view some of the many zombie movies or series that had been released over the years might bizarrely help educate us and maybe aid us in improving our tactics. But weirdly, I hadn't missed the flickering screen that most families resorted to for their entertainment. The children who had seemed so reliant on their electronic devices for entertainment hadn't moaned about the lack of them since it had all begun. They still had their iPads with them, but hadn't once asked if they could be charged, something we could easily have done using the generators we had or the power outlets in all the vehicles. It was as if they'd forgotten about them, but now with an impressively large television bolted to the wall, they seemed to be drawn to it like moths around a flame.

Sidling up to Becky after I'd stretched my back, which was aching from spending hours on my knees fighting with stubborn pieces of bed frame, I put my arm around her, as I could see her watching the children too.

"Shall we be cowards," I whispered conspiratorially "and let Maud regulate their TV time? They'll listen to her."

She chuckled as she rested her head against my shoulder, "I think as responsible parents, that would be the safest way to do it."

The ringing of the gong that Maud had found and begun using as the dinner bell drew us all to the dining room.

"They've cleared the main island!" Steve jubilantly announced when he returned from his nightly radio call to the fleet. Even though we were not part of the operation, we had still played a part in planning it and so his news brought us all to our feet and we celebrated with cheers, hugs and handshakes.

He waited for us to quieten down before he continued.

"Unfortunately, they lost a few in the fight, but that was in the initial stages before their experience and tactics improved and they adapted to the situation. The fleet in the Solent will remain in position until the smaller Isles are cleared, which they predict will take another few days. Then they plan to relocate there."

Pulling a list from his pocket, he studied it for a few moments before continuing.

"I now have the locations of all the places where personnel are still trapped, and they've tasked me with investigating the ones within our reach." He held up his hands for quiet as he could see a few of us about to ask questions. "If you could let me finish," he said gently, "what I propose is that tomorrow we try the motorway to see if we can secure a fuel truck and possibly some more food ones too. It will at least confirm to us what a resource we think the motorways with all their abandoned lorries on could be. If that's successful," he then looked at Chris and me, "then the day after tomorrow, I suggest we try and see if we can get our air force airborne. I've checked with the meteorologists at the fleet and they predict the weather will be calm, with good visibility for the next few days at least. After that, it's looking more unsettled for quite some time, so it could be a case of now or, if not never, then maybe later."

Pausing to judge our reaction, he smiled when he saw both of us nodding in eager agreement. Since I'd made my decision, my excitement about going flying again had been building and I couldn't wait to see if I could still do it.

"Now let's decide who amongst us will drive any lorries we find."

CHAPTER TWENTY

Once we'd all done Simon's group exercise class, which he now held every morning before breakfast, we all changed into our 'fighting clothes' and prepared to leave.

After performing a final check on the vehicles we were taking with us, those of us going on today's mission either climbed aboard Shawn's trailer or into the back of the armoured vehicle and we drove slowly out through the barbican entrance.

Much to their disgust, we'd chosen not to take any armoured knights with us since we didn't plan to be fighting hordes of zombies on foot today, just hopefully jumping into the cab of a lorry and driving it back. To their credit through, they wanted to go, armoured up or not, so to mollify them, some of them were chosen to go armed only with their close-quarter weapons and firearms. The rest were left on guard duty.

Steve promised them, though, that he envisaged them all being needed to go on the mission to the airfield the following day and he wanted them to be rested for that.

No zombies had been seen in the grounds since we'd fixed the holes in the perimeter fence and reinforced other areas we deemed a potential weak point. Nevertheless, as we drove slowly through the grounds to the gate, we all stood ready; just in case. Unfortunately, the main gate to the town was a different matter. The ones that had probably been attracted by our last mad dash through the town as we'd gathered the medical supplies were still gathered in stupid obstinance around the gate. Tripping over the piled-up bodies that had been swept aside by the ploughs, they shuffled around.

"Shit!" Steve broadcast over the radio, his voice sounding apologetic. "Maybe we do need the knights, after all. Sorry chaps, I clearly didn't think this through enough."

Woody spoke next, his cheerful voice gently mocking his superior. "Bugger me, guys, we have a Rupert who can admit he's made a mistake," he said, referring to the common derogatory nickname the rank and file in the military gave to their officers. "Don't worry, *Sir*. We can deal with this lot from here, I reckon. But may I suggest we ask Willie to bring his trailer up with a few knights on board so they can keep the entrance clear while we're gone."

I could hear the humour in his voice as he replied, "Good idea, Sergeant. If you could get him to do that, we'll start thinning them out a bit while we wait."

Shawn, with his usual companion, Louise, by his side in the tractor, pulled the vehicle forwards, angling it so that those of us in the trailer could bring our weapons to bear more easily.

Without being asked to, we all put our main weapons down and picked up one of the silenced .22 rifles that were stacked in the weapons bin on the trailer. We all agreed there was no point in attracting more zombies by making any more noise than we needed to. Inserting a loaded magazine into my chosen rifle, I pulled and pushed the bolt back and forth to chamber one of the small subsonic bullets, and resting it on the side of the trailer to steady my aim, I began firing.

By the time Willie pulled up in his tractor with six armoured knights aboard its own trailer, we'd shot most of the ones in our sight. Jamie was the first to climb down and walk towards the gate. He had a big smile on his face when he looked up smugly at Steve as he passed.

"Don't need us, *don't* you? Thought you could handle those big scary zombies out there all by yourself, *did* you?"

Geoff grinned just as broadly as Jamie when he joined him at the gate and they both peered theatrically through the it at the few that were still staggering around, before turning back to us.

"Well!" Geoff said. "It looks like you managed without us after all. Do you want us to head back? I was just brewing a pot of tea before your cry for help had us rushing to your aid. We do need our rest after all, don't you know."

Steve, standing on the wheel arch of the armoured car, raised his hands in mock surrender, and replied just as humorously, "Okay, chaps, you got me. There's no need to go on about it too much, though." He then waved towards the gate. "If I could trouble you to open the gate and keep any more that appear under control until we get back, I would be most grateful."

Jamie called to the other four knights, who had climbed down from Willie's trailer by now. "Come on, lads, they do need us after all. On me, boys."

Every element of humour and light-heartedness vanished from the knights as they gathered around Jamie and Geoff at the gate. It was game time and they knew it. The time for banter and messing about was over.

Jamie issued a few commands and the knights formed a line behind him with their shields held ready as he fiddled with the code lock that secured the gate. Once he'd removed the lock, he slid back the bar and with a pull, he heaved the gate back on its hinges. Stepping back, he hefted his own shield and the line opened up to add him to the middle of the pack. Another command issued from his throat and keeping formation, they advanced, axes and swords swinging and thrusting at any that lay on the ground to ensure they were permanently dead, before stepping over them as they headed for the ones further away. Within minutes, all within reach were dispatched. He waved his arm as he indicated for us to drive towards him.

He called up to us as we passed, bumping over the few bodies lying in our path,

"Don't worry, we'll keep it clear here. Just radio us when you're on your way back and we'll open the gates for you."

We all shouted our thanks to them as we went past. They stood leaning on their shields, gathering their breath after their exertions and offered a few ribald comments in return. Driving in line, we gathered speed and drove towards the nearby motorway junction. Everyone aboard knew what vehicles we were looking for, so as soon as we drove down the motorway slip road, we lined the sides of the trailer, eager to spot our first find. Having driven up this section of motorway only a few days ago when we led the zombies out of the town, we knew that the few miles of road contained several abandoned lorries. It was what was in them we did not know.

Louise's voice sounded through the radio when Shawn slowed the tractor as we approached the first lorry. "Shawn says we'll try this one first. Get ready, everyone."

The plan we'd come up with was, as all the best ones were, simple. It was easier to get in and out of the armoured car, so it made sense for the ones in the trailer to provide cover for them as they disembarked and inspected the vehicle.

Everyone in the trailer stood with their weapons ready as the rear door on the armoured car opened and the four inside stepped out and approached the nearby lorry. I noticed that the unfortunate driver of the lorry was still trapped in its cab and the noise of our arrival had awoken it from whatever stupor the weakened zombie brain went into when there were no external influences to stimulate it. It was now banging its head against the side window and its decaying hands left smears of gore streaked down it. The driver must have been trapped in the cab since the very beginning and the sun beating down on it would have turned it into an oven in the daytime. I thought it must have once been on the obese side of the diet spectrum and the daily broiling it had been receiving had not been kind to its body. It looked bloated to the point of bursting and when it pressed its hands against the window, pieces of skin, flesh and blood remained stuck to the hot glass.

It was not a pleasant sight and from the exclamations of disgust from the others by my side, I wasn't the only one whose attention was caught by the gruesome display.

Telling myself off for allowing my attention to be drawn to something that wasn't an immediate danger to any of us, I looked towards the rear of the articulated lorry. Using bolt croppers, the padlock had been removed from the locking bar and the rear doors swung open. One of the group climbed inside to emerge moments later shaking his head.

"It's full of wheelbarrows," he shouted disappointedly. Eddy, beside me on the trailer, pulled a notepad from his pocket and wrote down the number plate of the truck and what it contained. What the lorry carried might not be useful to us now, but we'd sensibly decided to write down what we found in case we needed whatever we discovered later.

Eddy put the notepad back into his pocket before lifting his rifle and shooting the unfortunate lorry driver through the head, ending his solitary zombie life forever.

"Okay," called Steve to us all cheerfully, "it was never going to be that easy, was it? Climb back onboard, everyone, and let's try the next one."

The next three lorries revealed nothing of immediate interest to us, but their contents were noted down all the same. Shawn was also looking out for tell-tale signs of a big aerial on lorries, indicating they probably had a CB radio fitted and when he saw one, we stopped and he quickly removed the unit and the aerials from them until we amassed a small collection.

"That's better," I exclaimed with delight when the next lorry we came across was emblazoned with the name of a well-known supermarket. "Let's hope it was on the way to drop off and not the other way around." I continued with an air of forced hopefulness.

The door to this lorry's cab was open, which was good news because if it held what we hoped it did, it meant we wouldn't have the driver to deal with as well. There was a mutual holding of breath, as we all watched the padlock being cut and the door opened. The shouts of delight we all heard from the ones by the doors made us all cheer happily, because even though we couldn't see what it contained, we could tell from their reaction that it was clearly good news.

"It's full," Steve shouted, this time sounding genuinely happy and not echoing the forced tone he'd been putting on at our previous disappointments. He helped to close the door and then slapped the side of the vehicle with his hand as he called out, "Let's get this bad boy started up and get back home." Then he turned to Steve and Jim. "Do you want to drive this one back? I'll let some of my lads drive the next one so you can all have a play at being truckers."

"Yes, Sir!" they both sounded in unison and with big grins on their faces at the excitement of having the chance to drive the lorry, ran off towards the cab.

"Bloody kids," exclaimed Eddy by my side. "Just look at 'em both." As they ran, they were arguing over who was going to drive, neither wanting to concede and let the other have a go before they did. Until they were stopped by a sharp command from Eddy.

"Marine Ellis. You will drive this time and will let Marine Popley do so next time. Now children, we haven't got all day so stop fucking about and get on with it."

Brought slightly more under control, they both gave a cheeky salute and Jim climbed up into the cab. "Great, it's still got the keys in the ignition." He shouted out loud in delight after a few moments of searching. If the keys had been missing, it wouldn't have been much of a problem as Shawn had told us he'd be able to bypass the key and hotwire vehicles if necessary.

Unfortunately, when Jim turned the key, nothing happened. The battery on the lorry was dead. This was another event we'd planned and prepared for, because we'd known that if the vehicle was abandoned as this one was, the driver would probably not have turned off the engine, because he'd have had far more terrifying things on his mind at the time, like just getting out of the cab as fast as he could and fleeing. The lorry would then have sat there with its engine running until it ran out of fuel and then with the electrics still on, the battery would have drained.

Knowing this, we'd brought jerry cans full of diesel with us and the heavy-duty battery booster we'd loaded at the vehicle maintenance area at Bickley Barracks. It was one of the many items we'd hurriedly loaded as others kept the horde of zombies at bay. We'd known at the time it might be useful in the future and we were very glad we had it now.

If the lorry had run out of fuel, in all probability the engine would need the air bleeding from the valves. Chris knew how to do this from his experience operating lorries as a builder's merchant, so we'd naturally included him in the team. He was in the trailer with us, already with the spanners he would need in his pocket.

I called over to Steve. He was standing with the other occupants of the armoured car by the cab, with their weapons held ready, scanning the surroundings, ready for any zombies who had yet to make an appearance on our quiet stretch of road. We all knew with dreaded certainty that eventually, they would if we didn't move soon.

We didn't lower the ramp but opened the rear door on the trailer and as Chris jumped down and headed to the front of the lorry, Eddy and I lowered the heavy booster pack and jerry cans into the waiting arms.

While one broke off the lorry fuel filler cap and poured in some diesel, another was connecting the cables to the right terminals on the battery. Chris, who had lifted the engine cover up on the lorry, then told Jim to turn on the ignition. With power now connected, the starter motor turned over. I couldn't see what Chris was doing as he stood on the lorry's front bumper and leaned into the engine bay, but as Jim kept the engine turning, it began to cough and splutter until eventually, with a roar and a cloud of black smoke from the exhaust, the engine fired up and with a few revs from Jim's foot pressing on the accelerator pedal, ran smoothly.

Everyone cheered again. Once more, we'd worked together, using our combined skills and knowledge to overcome events. Steve, not wanting to delay any more, whirled his arms in the air to indicate to everyone to get back on board and shouted to be heard over the engine noise, "Let's roll, everyone." Chris slammed the engine cover shut and Eddy and I reached down to help him back into the trailer, as the others hauled the battery booster into the back of the armoured car to save lifting it up to us.

The lorry was already pointing in the right direction as we'd been driving the wrong way down the motorway for this very purpose and it pulled in behind us after we'd turned around, and in convoy, we headed the few miles back to the castle.

At the gates the knights had done a good job of keeping the area clear and opened them when we told them via the radios we were approaching. With barely a pause, the plough smashed through the few new piles of corpses they'd created in our absence and we continued through the grounds. The lorry was too large to attempt to fit through the barbican, so once we'd driven inside, we backed it up to the entrance and after a few cups of tea and a debrief on the mission, we organised its unloading.

'Many hands make light work' is the expression. But after a few hours of lifting and carrying, we were all glad when the last few items were offloaded onto Woody's trailer. Woody drove up to the main entrance door for the other team to carry the stuff inside and stack it in the store rooms under Maud's direction. She was standing at the door armed with a clipboard to note down everything that was unloaded and then she told the porters where she wanted it stored.

Following a quick lunch, we gathered in the Great Hall to discuss the next item on our wanted list: fuel. The mission to gather more food had been a success and we now had the confidence to venture further down the motorway until we found a fuel lorry. Not much more planning was required as we just needed to repeat what we'd done before and as the tactics had worked, there was no need to change them at all.

With a wave at the ones staying, the knights on Willie's trailer led us out through the barbican to the castle entrance once more. The plan was that they would then stay and guard the gates while we were gone.

Much later that evening, we popped a few corks on one of the many bottles of champagne we'd scavenged from the lorry and celebrated a successful day. Two more lorries full of food and a tanker that contained both petrol and diesel were parked in the grounds outside the walls, awaiting unloading.

As we sat around chatting and laughing, darkness falling outside, Shawn held two DVDs in the air. "Which training video shall we watch tonight?" he asked as he showed us two zombie movies he'd selected.

CHAPTER TWENTY-ONE

"What's the matter, darling?" Becky asked as she watched me getting changed out of my exercise gear in the morning. "You've been quiet since we got up."

Once again, I couldn't hide anything from my wife, a fact she always reminded me of.

"Nothing much, love," I said quietly, trying to hide my emotions a little more. "It's just that now it's going to happen, I'm a bit nervous about today and this flying business." I shrugged. "It's been years since I flew and there's a lot that can go wrong. Who knows if we'll be able to find a working plane and then will we be able to navigate around and then land safely? I just don't know now if it's a good idea at all."

She walked up to me and put her arms around me, smiling. "Don't tell me Maverick is getting scared now. It's all you and Chris have talked about since it was decided. Regaling us with all your stories of bravely soaring through the air until, to be honest, I think you started boring us."

I looked at her, shocked. "Me? Boring? They were good stories. Weren't they?" I said indignantly but knowing that in all fairness it was probably true. Both Chris and I had talked like excited schoolboys about to go on an adventure and little else, once we had decided to give it a go.

"Yes, dear, they were," she replied in her usual 'if you say' so voice. "But now that you mention it, I think Chris was looking a bit nervous, too, earlier on. Maybe you two should go and have a chat about it and decide if you really want to go ahead with it. It's not too late to back out, you know, and trust me, if you decide not to go, no one will think any the worse of you for it."

Silently, I donned my clothes as I thought about what she'd said. I was nervous, but was it trepidation or real fear that was making my guts churn? She was right, I needed to have a word with Chris before it was too late.

Chris answered when I knocked on the door to his room. Taking one look at my face, he smiled grimly and said, "You too?"

"Yes, mate. Now we're actually going to try it, I'm bricking myself, if I'm honest about it. Can I come in and have a chat with you out of earshot of everyone else?"

"Of course," he replied, opening the door fully and waving me in. "Nicky's here, shall I ask her to leave?" Nicky emerged from the bathroom as I entered the room.

"No," I replied. "After all, it does concern her too, so she should be here." Their room was one of the suites that the place rented to people who wanted to experience staying in the splendour of a castle and was luxuriously appointed. He led me into the sitting room and indicated for me to sit in a chair. Nicky joined Chris on the sofa opposite me.

"Nice room," I opened with, trying to think of how to start the conversation. Not being able to come up with anything other than to be direct, I came out with it. "Are you as nervous about today as me?"

I looked at both of them in the silence that followed until Chris spoke.

"Frankly, mate, yes I am," he eventually replied. "There's no instructor sitting by our side who can take over if something happens up there. It's just going to be me and you up there and no disrespect, but we don't know really how good either of us is."

I nodded in agreement. "You ain't wrong there, pal," I replied. "It's a risk and I was well up for it before, but now the time's getting close, I'm having second thoughts and it looks like you are as well."

"I certainly am," he answered "But the way I'm thinking, I reckon we should try anyway. The place may be completely overrun for all we know, or there might not even be a suitable plane for us to use, but if we don't try, we won't know. Why don't we try as planned? We can start by doing a few circuits of the field and maybe a bit of touch and go." He was referring to the training routine of flying around the landing pattern of the airfield, landing and taking off again in one manoeuvre, to repeat it again and again. It was usually the first solo flights you did as a novice.

I smiled at him, remembering the nervous moment the instructor had stepped from the plane for the first time and let me loose on my own. I mulled it over for a moment before replying, "I suppose if you put it like that, it's nothing we haven't both done before, and at least we'll have each other to remind ourselves what to do."

I looked him in the eye. "Are you happy to give it a go?"

He looked at Nicky, who took his hand in hers and nodded to him. He smiled, "Well, the boss says okay, so let's do it. And look out the window, the weather's about as good as it can get for flying."

I stood and shook his hand, grinning in relief. If he'd been as nervous as me, it was a good sign. We would both be taking it very seriously and not letting overconfidence or complacency mar our judgment to the detriment of safety.

"Okay, mate, let's go and get ready with the others." Then I couldn't help myself and added now that my nerves had faded a little, "But I'm still Maverick."

***

Steve and his sergeants planned to use most of us for the mission. Five soldiers would stay behind to protect the castle, supported by all the children as sentries who would be overseen by Maud, Charles the vicar and Nicky, because her pregnancy ruled her out of going anywhere dangerous, by universal agreement. Everyone else was told to arm up and get ready to leave.

The airfield at Wellesbourne was only about fifteen minutes' drive away under normal circumstances and we didn't expect it to take much longer than that as we knew the vehicles we were taking could plough through most things we came across.

Waving goodbye to those remaining, after we'd loaded the last few items onto both Willie's and Shawn's trailers, both tractors and the armoured car drove once more through the castle grounds to the world beyond our sanctuary. Only a few more zombies had gathered at the entrance gate and they were quickly dispatched, although the smell emanating from the piles of rotting corpses surrounding it reminded us that we needed to do something about them, or they would become a health hazard. I looked horrified as swarms of rats scattered from our engine noise, skittering away to dive down drains or into the undergrowth.

Grim looks were exchanged. All the rotting the corpses would make ideal conditions for an explosion in the rat population as food for the voracious scavengers was now plentiful, combined with no local authority anymore to deal with it. Only us.

Another item to add to the list, I thought grimly.

The airfield was a former World War two base that had survived the closures and now operated as a private airfield for light aircraft. Several flying schools operated from it, including the one I'd used all those years ago. Following my directions, we skirted around the village that bore the airfield's name and drove down the road that accessed it.

The area was eerily quiet, we'd only encountered a few undead on the journey and they'd been dealt with in the usual way; either by being run over or stabbed with a spear. Thanks to the castle, we now had a range of better spears, rather than the tried and trusted sharpened metal stakes we'd previously been using. The long hardwood-handled lances and boar spears that had adorned the walls of the castle proved once again that ancient weapons now had a firm place in the world we were living in. Training had already begun under the tutelage of the knights, on using them as well as the heavier pikes, which some had found too cumbersome to wield. We were all learning and inventing new and better ways for us to fight our new enemy.

The main carpark was thankfully deserted as our convoy drove into it. I suppose on the morning the apocalypse exploded across the United Kingdom, the last thought on anyone's mind was to go for a pleasure flight.

I smiled nostalgically as I recognised the building that housed the flying school I'd used, remembering the many happy hours spent there.

All the drivers had been given instructions, including my roughly drawn map of the place, and knew where to go. Shawn stopped the tractor right outside the entrance to the building as the others pulled up alongside to protect us.

"Okay, guy's, let's do this," I said to everyone in the trailer. The knights were first down the ramp once we'd lowered it into position and formed up around the door. A few blows from Geoff's mace destroyed the lock and with a kick from him, the door swung open. After they'd entered and checked that the building contained no surprises, they waved me in. The place hadn't changed in the years of my absence, so I went straight for the key safe where I knew I'd find the keys to their planes.

It wasn't a heavy duty safe, only designed to keep all the keys in one place and it easily yielded to the crowbar I'd brought with me for this very purpose. Handily, all the keys had the model and unique registration codes of their relevant aeroplane on their labels and I sorted through them until I found several keys indicating they belonged to the type of plane that both Chris and I used to train in. We'd both chosen to use the larger four-seater low wing type rather than the smaller, more cramped two-seater high wing type. I knew the flying school had once had at least four of the type and when I was taking lessons, we used whichever one was available. The cockpit displays varied between them but the controls were all similar and so it didn't matter which one we would use.

Once I had the keys, I searched for and found the maintenance log for the planes, hanging on a hook next to the key box. Of the three planes for which I'd found keys, one was reported in for maintenance, but two were available to fly. Looking through the window of the office that fronted the airfield, I tried to see the planes but couldn't pick them out from the many that sat on the grass by the taxi way.

Opening cupboards, I soon found two headsets, a small folder and a laminated map. I stuffed them all into a bag I found and told the knights I had what I needed, and it was time to leave. I knew that the gate at one end of the carpark led to the airfield. The knights accompanied me, their armour chinking metallically as they walked beside me. A padlock secured it, but Jamie soon removed it with a cordless angle grinder he pulled from a bag he was carrying. Seconds later, I'd opened the gate and all the vehicles drove onto the airfield. I closed it and the knights joined me to jog beside the slow-moving vehicles until they came to a stop next to the airfield's small control tower.

The benefit of good planning showed once those chosen for the next task had disembarked from the vehicles and formed their allocated groups, and we began phase two of the operation. While Wille drove his tractor with a team onboard the trailer around the entire airfield to check the whole place out, Shawn headed to the control tower, accompanied by two knights. Their job was to see if they could get the radio operational so that when Chris and I were flying, we could stay in contact. Chris and I, accompanied by a force of both knights and soldiers, went to find and inspect the planes.

Calling out the registration code for them, we walked down the lines of planes until we identified the two we were looking for. When we inspected them, one was easily our preferred choice. It was newer and had more up-to-date displays and instruments on the cockpit. With the others keeping watch, we inspected it carefully. As you would expect from a fully maintained flying school plane, everything seemed to be in good order. The log I had with me stated it had flown the day before the apocalypse hit, and the last act of the now probably dead or turned instructor was to top off the fuel tanks so it would be ready for the next day.

To be sure, we dipped the tanks in both wings and confirmed they were full.

I handed Chris the keys and the bag I'd filled and said, "Let's see if we can start this baby, shall we? I'll keep everyone away from the prop."

Warning the others to stand clear, I watched as he climbed on board and began the starting sequence. After a few minutes, the starter motor whirred, and the propeller began it's familiar stuttering, rotating as the engine turned over. The engine coughed a few times but after twenty seconds of trying, it failed to start. I wasn't worried; aeroplane engines were fickle beasts at the best of times and never liked starting from cold. I remembered a few times my instructor virtually flattening the battery attempting to start one until it eventually kicked into life.

Chris released the key, stopping the starting process, and fiddled with various settings on the cockpit before retrying. This time it sounded better as soon as he turned the key and soon the engine caught cleanly, and after Chris raised the revs for a few seconds, he pulled back the throttle and it steadied back to idle.

I could not help but cheer as the familiar engine sound excited me. I wasn't worried or scared any more, but desperate to get in the air.

Willie drove towards us down the taxi way after completing his circuit of the airfield and I walked up to his cab. He turned off the engine and opened the door so he could speak to me.

"It's all clear, laddie. The fence around the place has kept them out. A few can be seen wandering about beyond it and I'm sure all this noise we're making will attract them, but I don't think there are enough of them to worry us at the moment." He looked at the plane that sat with its engine running and propeller turning. "You all set to go, then?" he asked with a grin. At my nod, he replied, "Rather you than me, my boy. I prefer to keep two feet on the ground now. I've spent more time than I like to remember sitting in the back of falling apart helicopters and planes, expecting to hit the next mountain, to be bothered with flying anymore."

"Thank for the confidence boost," I replied sarcastically and then turned as I spotted Shawn running towards me.

"Radio's operational. All we had to do was wire it up to the genny we brought with us." He, too, looked at the plane and asked the same question, "You good to go, then?"

"Yes, mate," I replied, shrugging, nerves once more showing on my face after Willie's comments had reminded me of the potential dangers once more. "I don't think we can put it off anymore."

"You'll be fine," he answered with more confidence than I felt and handed me a slip of paper. "It's the frequency of the airfield. I'll head back to the tower and we can do a comms check before you go." He slapped me on the back as he turned and ran back to the tower.

I looked at the scrap of paper and recognised the frequency he'd written on it. It was the one I'd tuned the radio into many times in the past and I was surprised at my recollection of it.

Chris was in the left-hand pilot's seat already with his headset on as I climbed in and put my rifle on the back seat, before sitting down in the right-hand seat and closing the door. The engine noise was muffled slightly, but he handed me my set of headphones he'd already plugged into the cockpit. Knowing it was easier to talk with them on, I waited until I'd fitted them before speaking.

"All set, mate?" I asked as I reached for the radio and turned it on.

"As good as we can be," he answered with a nervous smile. Happily spotting that the radio was already turned to the correct frequency, I pressed the button to set the radio to broadcast on the control column and spoke.

"Maverick to tower. Can you hear me? Goose has the stick and is ready to fly."

Shawn's voice immediately replied, "If you two think you can get away thinking you're in a Tomcat, when from here it looks like a child's toy, then good luck to you."

"Aw, come on man," Chris said, laughing. "Let us dream, can you?"

"Have it your way, you idiots," came the reply through our headsets. "We're reading you loud and clear. Let me just get everyone out of the way and then Steve will escort you to the runway."

This was the next part of the plan. We would be vulnerable on the ground so the armoured vehicle would stay close to us until we were airborne. They would then continue patrolling the airfield, keeping it clear until we returned.

"Give us five minutes to familiarise ourselves first, please," replied Chris.

"Good call," I said to him over the private channel. I looked at the displays, dials and controls on the cockpit in front of me. To the untrained eye, it would be a mass of unrecognisable, confusing instruments and initially they were to me until I spotted the location of the important ones first and then went through the rest, reminding myself of their use and function.

Then I remembered the folder and map I'd found when I was searching for the headsets. Seeing Chris had put the bag on the back seat, I reached over and pulled out my finds and showed them to Chris, who immediately said, "Good find, that'll help." The folder contained the standard preflight checklist, setting out in order the meticulous but standardised process you went through to ensure the plane was ready and fit to fly. Eventually we had gone through the list carefully and methodically; checking everything twice, just to be sure. We both studied the windsock to work out which runway to use and spent a few minutes studying the flight map to familiarise Chris with the area. I'd spent many hours flying around the region and knew that with today's excellent visibility, we could fly from landmark to landmark and probably not need the map at all, but it made sense to do so. I did try the satellite navigation system, but it disappointingly, though not unexpectedly, didn't work. Chris looked at me. "Ready mate?"

"Yes," came my one-word reply.

He pressed the broadcast button. "Shawn we're ready. We'll go right and use that runway." To emphasise that fact and knowing Shawn was most likely studying us through binoculars, I pointed in the direction we needed to go.

"Okay, guys," he replied immediately, "Steve is ready to escort you."

CHAPTER TWENTY-TWO

Between ourselves, we'd agreed that Chris should attempt the first take-off, since he was the one with the more recent flying experience. I sat quietly by his side with my hands away from the controls as he applied power, and the aircraft picked up speed.

In no time, the familiar sensation of leaving solid ground made me smile. As we gained altitude, I felt my confidence return as memories kicked in. The plan was to perform a few circuits of the airfield to build our confidence and then we would practise a few touch-and-gos and if we were still happy, we would begin the mission.

I looked across at Chris. His face was set in a frown of deep concentration and I could see the whites of his knuckles as he held the steering column in a vice-like grip. I patted him on the leg.

"Well done, mate," I said as I got his attention and he glanced towards me. "Now let's do a few circuits of the airfield."

I could see the tension flood from him at my reassurance and his grip on the column loosened and his face changed to one of accomplishment and relief.

"Thanks, pal," he replied. "Do you want to take over?"

"No, mate, not yet, you're doing just fine. Let's stick to the plan and I'll observe you for a while to fully refresh myself," I said, my voice now full of the confidence I could feel growing inside.

Twenty minutes later, we'd both completed a few circuits of the airfield and practised a few touch-and-go landings each until we were as confident as we could be that we could fly further afield. The visibility was excellent, and I'd marked on an Ordinance Survey map the location the Royal Navy wanted us to investigate first to see if the rescue missions they hoped to undertake for the personnel trapped in them were viable.

While we were flying, we kept a continual conversation going with Shawn and the others who were monitoring the radio in the airfield's tower. We both took the compliments about how smooth our landings had been with a pinch of salt, as I knew mine in particular had been a little bouncy.

With the map held in my hands, I checked the compass on the control panel and compared it with the handheld one I had pressed against the map.

"If we use Warwick as our marker," I said, with my brow once more furrowed with concentration, "I'll call out landmarks and bearings as I see them. Does that sound a good idea, Chris?"

"Sure," he replied, "the castle will be a great marker." He smiled as he continued, "And if we do a fly-by, it'll let them know we at least managed to take off."

"You mean it'll stop Nicky worrying, more like."

"Yes, alright then," he signed theatrically, "that too. Okay then, navigator, point me in the right direction, my good fellow," he commanded, adopting his poshest Royal Airforce accent. I looked out of the window and pointed at the town of Warwick, distant but clearly visible from our height.

"That way, my dearest chap," I replied, mimicking his accent.

The plane banked and we left the airfield behind.

I waved out of the window at Stanley and Daisy, who had climbed to the highest tower on the castle along with the rest of the children when we'd first flown overhead. Our young audience looked up and waved their arms about in excitement.

Chris had slowed down as much as he could and was flying a number of slow, banked circuits of the castle while I was using my phone, which I'd charged for this purpose, to take pictures of the castle so we could study our new home from a different viewpoint and maybe see any improvements we could make.

I took control for the last circuit so Chris could wave at Nicky, who was standing in the middle of the courtyard waving back as excitedly as everyone else. Having already worked out our required heading and with a last few dips of the wings, I settled the plane on its new course. With the slight crosswind that was blowing across our nose, we knew we would have to make frequent adjustments to compensate for it and so needed to judge our progress using landmarks and the maps Chris, as the current navigator, had laid on his lap to pinpoint our current position as we flew over them.

I increased and lowered our altitude until we reached a height we both agreed gave us the best view of the land below us and the horizon in front of us, so we could plot a good way ahead to make navigation easier. We didn't want to miss any signs of survivors.

With every minute that passed, my confidence grew and the more I relaxed. I was genuinely enjoying myself and found it impossible to keep the smile off my face. Flying over Birmingham erased it, though. Spotting the landmark of Warwickshire County cricket ground, on an impulse I turned towards it, reducing height and speed and once overhead, banked in the direction of my house, which was close to it.

My road was easy to find as it backed onto a park and I soon spotted it. Flying over the area, I was horrified as I looked down to see a lot of burnt-out houses and the dark shapes of massed zombies filling the area.

"My God!" I exclaimed as I pointed my house out to Chris. "Can you take a few pics, mate? I need to show Becky this when we get back." I remained silent as he took photo after photo of the desolation that was once the nice suburb of Moseley, where I used to live. My house seemed to have escaped the fires that had ravaged many, but it was clearly a dead area. It was once so vibrant and full of life, now it was home to only the undead who filled every street.

"It looks like going on holiday saved our lives in more ways than one," I said quietly, trying to rationalise the devastation below me. "We wouldn't have made it if we'd woken up to, that would we?"

"Face it, mate," replied Chris seriously. "You would probably have caught the virus or whatever caused it, anyway." He paused as he looked out of the window before he added softly, contemplating how he himself had survived the outbreak, "It's down to luck for all of us. You were on holiday; we spent the night at home and didn't go to work in the morning because of the hospital appointment. All of us are here because of luck, fate or whatever you want to call it. Now we have to make the best of it and do our best to carry on."

We both fell silent as we looked at the ruined city five hundred feet below us. Eventually Chris spoke again, speaking as cheerfully as he could to try and alleviate the anguish he could see I was going through. "Come on, Maverick. There's nothing we can do about it now, so let's continue the mission." He inspected the map before calling out the bearing we needed to take. Keeping an eye on the compass, without saying a word in case my emotions beat me once more, I banked the plane and flew on, leaving my old home and life behind us, most likely never to see it again.

**

"Down there!" Chris exclaimed excitedly, twenty-five minutes later as we flew over open countryside. He pointed out of the window and I dipped the wing on the plane so I could see where he was pointing.

A farmhouse, standing solitary amongst open fields below us, had smoke coming from one of its chimneys. I reduced speed and altitude and headed towards it while Chris studied it through binoculars.

"They've got barricades on all the entrances. Looks like we have survivors," he reported as we got closer.

"Okay, let's try and get their attention," I said as I adjusted the throttle and other controls to set the plane up to fly circuits around it. "Have you got it on the map?"

He traced his finger across the page on the map open on his knees until he stabbed at a spot. With a pen he pulled from his pocket, he circled the small dot of a farm that was marked on the ordinance survey map before replying, "Got it. Looks in a remote spot as well."

On the second circuit, we both saw at the same time a group run from the main building, all staring up into the air at us. "We've got their attention. Let's see if they're friendly or not," Chris said. Not sure how we were going to do that from three hundred feet, I kept quiet and concentrated on flying a circular pattern around the sprawling farm buildings, casting occasional glances below me at the now growing crowd that stared back up at us.

"They're waving, at least," reported Chris as he waved back. He reached into the back of the plane and grabbed the pack he'd brought with him. Unzipping it, he pulled out a notepad and began writing on it. His plan how to deliver the message became clear when he rolled it up and pushed it into an empty water bottle he'd also retrieved from the pack.

"Want me to fly overhead?" I asked.

"Yes, please," he then spoke in his awful posh accent, "Message in a bottle ready for delivery, Maverick. He slid back the small window by his side." And added, "Bomb bay doors open. Begin bombing run, please."

I levelled the plane and headed straight for the house as he held his arm out of the window, with the bottle clutched tightly in his hand.

"Spot on!" he shouted with delight after he'd released it and watched it fall. "Right on the button. Now let's carry on to our destination. We're burning fuel flying around in circles like this."

"Don't you want to see if they've read it?" I asked.

"They have it. I told them we would be back overhead in about an hour and to find a way to reply."

When I didn't reply, he continued, "I asked if they were safe and needed help. I didn't tell them where we were because I think we need to know if they're good guys or not first. But I did say we were a group in a secure location with plenty of supplies. I'll get two different replies ready. Whichever one we use will depend on how they respond. Basically, one will wish them well and the other will tell them we'll attempt to reach them as soon as we can."

"Good idea," I answered. "What are they? A few hours away from us by road, at most, so it's well within our capabilities to get to them." Then I looked ahead at the mountains of Wales that were visible on the distant horizon. "Anyway, let's try and find the main reason we're up here and check out this army base."

As I knew the area and was more familiar with the landmarks that would aid our navigation, Chris took a turn at the controls while I kept us on the right course.

Thirty minutes later, he began circling the plane once more, this time over what looked to be a large sprawling military base. Following the instructions Steve had been given, we identified the building that we reckoned contained the bunker holding the trapped personnel. We could easily have found it without any instruction, though, as the area surrounding the building was thick with zombies. It was anyone's guess why they were still there. Maybe they'd followed others as they tried to reach it and nothing had drawn them away, or possibly through some remaining combined memory held in diseased brains, they collectively knew the area contained more living. It was clear, though, that whoever was inside was trapped and in a hopeless position unless rescue arrived.

Reporting our findings to Steve and with nothing else to see, we circled the base a few times so I could take more pictures, then we set our course back to the farmhouse to find out if the survivors there had replied.

"Inventive," I said, impressed as I saw they'd used sheets or towels to write a message on the ground in the yard of the farmhouse. I read it out aloud as Chris concentrated on flying.

"Ten. Safe. Low food."

It was a simple but concise message. Circling, I could make out ten people staring back up at us, all waving their arms above their heads. Through the binoculars, I could see joy, hope and excitement on all the faces.

My summary was an easy one to make, from what I was seeing below me.

"They seem to be all ages; I would guess they're the owners, by the look of them. They look like good guys to me. What do you think?" When he agreed, as I'd expected him to, I reached for the two messages Chris had already written. After reading them both, I selected the one informing them we would try to reach them as soon as we could and rolled it up to push into another water bottle we'd finished for this very purpose.

"Why don't we drop them the food we've brought with us as well?" Chris suggested. "It's not a lot, but if they're running low, it's better than nothing."

I didn't need to reply it was a good idea, because it clearly was. Twisting in my seat, I reached over to grab Chris's pack, in which we'd placed a few tins and other foodstuffs to keep us going, if for some reason we were forced to make an emergency landing and had to wait for rescue to arrive, or in the worst case make it back to the castle on foot. Removing the extra ammunition he had in there, and a few other items which I left on the back seat, I pulled the bag over, laying it on my lap. After putting the bottle in, I zipped it closed. It was clearly too big to fit through the small window, so the only way to deliver it was to open the door and drop it as we flew over.

"Aim for the field in front of the house," I instructed Chris. "If this thing lands on someone's head, it'll kill 'em and that won't help much."

Smiling in reply, I waited with one hand holding the bag and the other holding the door of the plane open, struggling against the buffeting of the wind while at the same time watching our progress out of the window. Dropping a bag from a moving plane is clearly a skill taught through practice, as I left it too late and watched helplessly as it missed where I thought it would land by hundreds of meters and it bounced through the long grass of the field by the farm, eventually coming to rest against a dry stone wall.

"Good shot," Chris said sarcastically as he dipped his wing and we both looked down at the three people running towards where it had ended up. "I hope they like dented cans and burst open packets because I think that's all they'll get from the rucksack."

I looked at him and was about to reply haughtily in an attempt to defend my poorly aimed bag drop when I saw the cheeky grin on his face. Choosing to reply with a one-word answer and not wanting to open myself up to any more friendly ribbing, I turned my attention to the map instead; tracing my finger over our intended route and looking out of the windows. "When do you think we'll be able to get to them?" Chris asked five minutes later.

"I don't see why we can't attempt it in the next few days, mate," I replied with a slightly distracted air, because my main concentration was on my continuous scanning of the ground below us as I searched for any other signs of life. I looked at the map on my lap and mentally planned the route between Warwick Castle and their location. "We know where they are, and I think we can avoid any big towns and villages if we choose country lanes. It'll take a fair few hours, I suppose, but it's nothing we haven't done before." I chuckled as my reply, so confidently condensed, registered in my brain. "Listen to me. I'm sounding like a bloody expert now, confidant we can navigate through miles of zombie-infested wasteland with no more trouble than going for a Sunday drive to a pub. The world has indeed gone mad."

"But, Tom, that is the point," Chris replied, his voice now serious. "We're doing amazingly well. Yes, we lost poor Daniel to those bastards and Marc has now got to come to terms with his injury, but apart from those devastating events, we *are* doing ridiculously well if you consider the situation. We have a secure location stocked with enough supplies to keep many more people than we currently number for a long time. Our safety is more than looked after by Steve and his men, let alone what we can do ourselves. The knights are enough to scare anyone to death on their own. And now look at us, flying around the country investigating the locations of other known forces at the behest of what remains of our armed forces, while they themselves are securing a land base on the Scilly Isles. And on our first attempt, we find another group who we're now talking calmly about offering help to. It's as if we're playing the heroes in some Hollywood movie or something." He waved his arm in front of him, indicating the countryside below us. "How many more will we help before some sort of normality gets restored? That's if it ever does."

I thought about what he'd said for a few moments before responding, "Yes, mate. I think someone out there has been looking after us all." I laughed mirthlessly before continuing. "A few weeks ago, when this all began, all I could think about was keeping my family alive for just the next few minutes, let alone the day. Now we're acting like the veterans I suppose we are, if you think about what we've all been through. I suppose the way I'm looking at it now is that, currently, my family are safe. We have the confidence and hard-won experience gained through doing and surviving things not one of us would have dreamed we were ever capable of, and as long as the risks are acceptable, we owe it to humanity to try and reach out to others. Take you, for example. If, by fate, we hadn't spotted you as we passed, I hate to say it, but you would probably be dead by now. Don't you owe it to humanity to pay it forward?"

"Absolutely, mate," he replied, his voice cracking with emotion. "Don't you think I'm not thankful every day for being saved by you? Now I'll get to hold my child in my arms, and I'll never be able to pay any of you back for that. Who knows what the world will be like in the months and years to come? But at least now I have a chance to live in it. And yes, I agree absolutely we do need to 'pay it forward' as you say. Now that we're so secure, what would it make us if we didn't try to help others?" Regaining his composure, he continued, "Now that's enough of me maudlin like an old woman, let's concentrate on getting back and on firm ground again." On our route, we circled a few likely looking properties where we thought survivors might be sheltering, but we found no more signs of life. Choosing not to fly over the city of Birmingham again, I'd set a course to fly us over the numerous towns and villages that surrounded the city, not in the hope of looking for survivors, but to try to see how many zombies they still held. Some looked reasonably empty, so we marked them as potential places we could gather supplies from in the future.

***

With the stall warning bleeping its familiar alert as i floated above the runway, I performed my best landing of the day and the plane gently made contact with the ground.

"Welcome back and nice landing," Shawn's voice sounded in our ears when he could see we were safely down and taxiing back to the main buildings. "We've cleared one of the hangers so we can secure the plane inside it, so if you follow Steve, he'll show you where to go; or do you want to refuel first?"

"Have you got the pumps working?" I asked. "If so, then yes, let's refuel now. It'll save time when we go up again."

"Of course," he replied with a sarcastic tone. "You may be the fancy fly boys, but where would you be without us mere mortals to keep everything working? Anyway, the tanks look almost full, so I don't think running out of avgas is something we'll need to worry about." He went silent for a moment. "I've just told Steve to stop at the refuelling point, so just follow him."

Twenty minutes later, we had the plane refuelled and pushed into the hanger, which we locked with a padlock Willie produced, and were heading home.

The evening turned into a celebration of another day of not only surviving but achieving another small victory against the world outside the safety of the walls. I suppose the existence we found ourselves living, any excuse for one was grabbed. Those who were rostered for lookout duty during the night didn't need to be told to limit their alcohol intake and they just sipped their drinks; although they still joined in just as enthusiastically as the rest of us. Chris and I were luckily excused guard duty by universal agreement, our efforts of the day generously deemed enough to warrant us a night off. Unfortunately, and probably due to the relief of surviving, I partook a little too much; it took Becky to help me to bed that night, helped by Willie, far more amused than she was.

***

The exuberant mood of the night before was replaced by silence at breakfast in the morning. Cups of coffee, paracetamol and silence seemed to be the cure that most people needed. Most sat in companionable silence and mutual suffering as we waited for Steve to complete the radio call he'd scheduled with the fleet.

CHAPTER TWENTY-THREE

The Scilly Isles

Captain Digby was exhausted as he stood on the quay at Hugh town, waiting for the boat to arrive that was going to ferry him out to the frigate that still stood in the bay. The outgoing tide had now washed away the remaining bodies that had been blocking it. While they'd been fighting in the town, the macabre pile of the undead had been cleared using grappling hooks thrown from some of the smaller, more manoeuvrable boats that had accompanied them. One by one, the by now bloating bodies had been pulled into the more open water of the harbour, where they had slowly drifted away on the tide.

He'd just declared successful the mission to clear St Mary's, the largest island in the Scilly Isles. Successful, but in his opinion costly.

Twenty men and women under his command had fallen to the zombies and he blamed himself for every one of those deaths, knowing it was down to his inexperience in dealing with a threat that no amount training or knowledge had prepared him for.

Unfortunately, the first few that had been bitten had been treated by their medics against all the advice they'd been given by those who had already fought them. They'd believed that their skills could save their friends and colleagues, despite what they'd been told. The results were as inevitable as they were shocking for those first experiencing it and more had been bitten when the patients had turned and attacked.

The initial confidence they'd felt after landing had soon disappeared, because no matter how good Captain Digby's tactics were, zombies kept managing to get close enough to attack. Ammunition soon ran out as entire magazines were emptied in panic to fell just one. Despite regular resupplies from the helicopters, whose coverage from their guns became impotent in the small streets and houses of the towns and villages, it soon became apparent that the best way to deal with zombies close up was to use the hastily manufactured melee weapons they all carried with them.

Through hard earned and costly experience, though, the rookie zombie fighters adapted and learned.

After witnessing the way the first few had turned when they were being treated, and not wanting anyone else to perform the task, Captain Digby had himself ended the lives of those bitten with a single shot to the head. A task that took a small piece of his soul away every time he pulled the trigger.

Stepping aboard the frigate, he headed straight for the command centre where he knew Admiral Walker-Jones was waiting for him to report on the mission.

The room went silent as the blood-stained and exhausted young officer walked in. The admiral strode up to him and extended his hand, his own crumpled uniform and drawn features showing the strain of command he was feeling.

"Good work, Captain Digby," he said simply.

Digby's voice cracked as he replied, "I failed, Sir. Too many were lost and I blame myself…" He stopped talking as the admiral held up his hand.

"No, you did not, Captain. You succeeded in your mission and the losses you received, however regrettable, were a price we had to pay." He looked at the pained expression on the young man's face, softened his tone and placed his hand on his shoulder. "Captain, you led your people well, and your losses reduced the more experience you gained. The fact you are mourning those who fell speaks volumes about your ability to command, young man. You were given a difficult task and you overcame the odds and won."

Digby looked him in the eye. "Sir. Thank you. But from the reports I've been given on those at Warwick Castle, they have not lost one of their number to zombies since this began and I thought we would do as well as them." Anger rose in him. "Despite all the training we receive, civilians have done better than us and that is not right. We are here to serve and protect our fellow countrymen. I…I…I'm having a difficult time coping with that, Sir."

The admiral smiled at his anguish. "I know, son. It's a strange world we find ourselves in, but we are in it, so we must do the best we can. I think those civilians at the castle have a lot they can teach us. The vehicles they've converted sound very interesting and it's definitely something we need to consider doing when we're planning our assault on the mainland."

His brow furrowed as more ideas raced through his head, then he turned to the others in the room. "Now, can we discuss moving the operation forward and clearing the rest of the islands? Our meteorologists are forecasting this weather will break soon and we need to get all our vessels, both naval and civilian, into safe anchorage. I have already ordered them to begin making their way here from the Solent and they will start arriving over the next few days. So time is of the essence."

He indicated for Digby to approach the large table in the room and they began planning phase two. As the meeting progressed, the captain's confidence in his ability grew, the experience he'd gained already showing in the input he made to the meeting, and the plan was soon agreed and preparations began once more.

He left to brief and prepare his exhausted troops for the next day's job.

The smaller islands, as surveillance from both the helicopter and boats had shown, indicated far fewer of the undead on all of them, which was a relief to all. Complacency, though, was never considered. The mission plan was similar to the one they had just completed. They would land in force and sweep each island from end to end in one large group. The helicopter would once more provide overhead coverage and resupply.

For obvious safety purposes, only those involved in the assault would be allowed to set foot on dry land until the missions were deemed successful. An extra full and very careful sweep of all the islands would then be undertaken before the all clear was given. They'd found from experience that even from houses and streets that had already been cleared or checked, an occasional zombie would emerge from a previously undiscovered hiding place. No one wanted to consider the possibility of what would happen if the infection were allowed to spread if an undiscovered zombie bit someone.

Warwick Castle

"They'll update us on the progress of the mission when they have more news, but they're confidant of success over the next few days," Steve ended his update for us from the fleet.

"What about the bunker?" I asked.

He smiled and handed me back my telephone, which we'd used to take photos as we flew over it.

"They thank you for your efforts yesterday. I described what you saw, and they will think about it once they've consolidated their position. The ones inside the bunker have enough supplies for a month at least, so there's no need to do anything rash for the time being.

They do want us to investigate the other sites, when the weather front they're expecting soon has cleared. Until then, we are to carry on as we are, consolidating our position and gathering what we can for the future. The news that you contacted other survivors was greeted with great relief. If we've found some, then there must be others, and in a way, it justifies the eventual mission plan."

"And what is that?" asked Becky, although she knew the answer.

Steve smiled at her and nodding his head in thanks at her for the prompt, replied, "To make the entire country zombie free, I imagine. Well it'd be a shame to go to all the effort if we were the only ones left, wouldn't it? Otherwise, they may as well just get themselves comfortable where they are and have a long holiday.

On one flight, you found another group, and as I just said, if there's one, there must be others."

He paused and looked at us all. "Once we've visited this group, I propose we actively begin searching for others by both land and air and offer help from the resources we've gathered, if they need it. Also, if we deem them suitable and their position is not safe, we bring them back here. To that end, we also need to continue gathering supplies and hopefully, more weapons. Not for us, but for those we meet."

Shawn interrupted him, "But Steve, I may have a hangover this morning and have missed the point. And please correct me if I am wrong, but isn't that what we've been doing pretty much since this whole thing started? So, what you are proposing is we carry on as we have been?"

After thinking about what Shawn had said for a moment, he replied, "Yes, of course it is. I think my head isn't too clear this morning either." He held his hands out in an expansive gesture. "What I propose is that we carry on as we have been until we hear differently. Is that okay with everyone?"

"Steve," Maud said sharply, "I agree, but may I remind you that we are doing what we are doing, not because some high and mighty officer tells us to. We are doing it because all of us here are decent human beings and not like those who killed poor Daniel. If you hadn't arrived, I can certainly assure you everyone here would be concentrating on extending the hand of help and friendship to any we came across. It may not be happening as quickly as it is now, but it would be."

Steve looked genuinely shocked and then contrite at her comment. "S…sorry, Maud," he stammered out his reply. "I know that, and I can assure you the fleet knows that too."

Then he sat down and looked exasperated, saying, "Can someone take over, please? The way my head is, I'm only going to say something stupid again and drop myself in it some more."

Maud stepped into the middle of the room and crossed her arms with determination. "Right then, young men. As you all look a little sorry for yourselves this morning, you can work off your hangovers by emptying the other lorries today. Tomorrow, we will go and reach out to those poor people at the farm."

At the thought of physical exercise there was a general groaning from most who were hoping for an easy day recovering from last night's celebrations, but Maud was not having any of it and continued.

"Looking at the state of most of you, I trust it will also be a lesson in overindulgence." She clapped her hands. "Now come on, then or will I have to get angry at you?"

Rueful looks were exchanged, and we all stood up and trooped outside to begin our day.

By the end of the day, both lorries had been emptied and the fuel lorry parked a safe distance away from the castle. Apart from exhaustion, most of us were feeling better. More rooms had to be cleared and allocated to allow for the extra supplies and Maud, helped by a few others, had catalogued and itemised everything we'd unloaded. We clearly had a lot of food, but as we knew, there was no point if we could gather more not to do so. After all, we didn't know how many people we would need to feed in the future.

The atmosphere was a lot more subdued that night as we watched another 'training video' before those not on guard duty went to bed earlier than usual.

CHAPTER TWENTY-FOUR

"Bloody hell," I moaned early the next morning as I carried another box of food up the ramp to put in the subfloor of the trailer. "We spent all day unloading it and now we seem to be carrying most of it back now." I looked at Maud, who was standing by the trailer checking items on a list she'd drawn up. "I know," I continued. "We don't know if they'll want to stay put or not."

Woody, who was stacking shotguns and rifles in the same trailer, along with boxes of ammunition for them, whispered at me conspiratorially, "Sssh, mate. I think we're still in trouble with Maud over last night. Let's be good boys until we leave and then we can moan about it."

We had planned to take three vehicles with us on the trip. The armoured car and tractor were included as always, but this time we decided to take Woody's Land Rover to use as a scout vehicle if we needed it. It still had its machine gun mounted on it, as did the trailer. None of the vehicles had encountered anything they couldn't deal with yet, so we were confident they were all suitable for the task ahead.

As soon as everything was stowed away securely, we joined the others, who were planning our route using a large map spread across the table in the dining room. Tracing my finger across the route, I could see Steve had planned it well. It zig-zagged across the countryside, missing a lot of towns and villages, all the time edging closer to the circle marking our eventual destination.

"What's the distance, Steve?" I asked as I stood up from leaning over the map to allow another to study it.

"About fifty miles or so," he replied. "Three hours at most, I reckon. But because we don't know what help these people might need, I think we should plan for an overnight stay. If we don't make it back today and as we'll be out of communication range, it'll stop everyone here worrying too much."

Not being able to argue with any of the choices he'd made, I nodded my head and checked my watch. "Shall we get moving then?" I stated. "Everything's loaded up and all the vehicles have been checked." I changed my voice to a poor imitation of a woman. "And as Maud would say, the sooner we leave, the sooner we'll be back."

Everyone smirked, but then I noticed no one was looking at me, but at the door behind me.

I cringed and my shoulders sagged as I said weakly, "She's right behind me, isn't she?"

"She is," came Maud's voice from behind me. I turned and she was standing in the doorway with her arms crossed. Her eyes betrayed the stern look on her face, they were glinting with mirth.

Full of embarrassment, I shuffled past her and gave her a peck on the cheek, muttering an apology in her ear.

Walking up the ramp of the trailer, I was surprised to see Charles, the vicar, already onboard. He was wearing body armour over his robes and had a rifle held in his hands. He hadn't previously been on any missions with us and was usually content with helping with the internal running of the castle and performing guard duty, along with looking after our spiritual wellbeing. His nightly prayers before dinner was served had quickly become a welcome tradition. They were more of a report on the day's activities, giving thanks for not only surviving, but achieving the goals we'd set ourselves. Delivered with humour and style, they were a joy to listen to. Often, he could be seen offering council or just a friendly ear to anyone who wanted to talk with him as he cheerfully went about his business.

"Charles, what are you doing?" I asked him.

"I haven't left the walls of the castle since we arrived," he began, "and I feel the need to see how the world has changed since then. Also, this group we're hoping to find might like to see a man of the cloth as well as you load of ruffians." He smiled kindly at me. "My flock isn't limited to just our group, it includes anyone who is still living through this dark pestilence that has befallen our beloved country, and it is my duty to offer my services to them all."

Ian, who had walked up the ramp behind me, had heard his little speech and he spoke before I could reply. "As long as you don't start singing *Onward, Christian Soldiers*, vicar, if you need to use your gun. I think that would be more than I could cope with. If only YouTube was still working, because that would get a gazillion hits."

Charles laughed out loud at his comment. "Now that is a fine rousing hymn. It's one of my favourites, in fact." With a look of joy on his face, he raised it to the heavens and began singing it. Once the gates were open the convoy left, with all of us waving to those staying, and we joined in with him as we dragged up the words from memories of long ago attended school assemblies and church services.

***

Aside from needing to clear the road of the occasional vehicle, the journey went to plan. The not unexpected zombies were dealt with as they shambled into our path and their bodies marked our route home like a gruesome trail of breadcrumbs. Unfortunately, the high hedges and poor signposting on country roads occasionally made navigation difficult. When a mistake was made, forcing us to make a U-turn, the complaints and moans we all communicated to Shawn, who was leading the way, were as good-natured as they were abusive, indicating the high spirits we were all in.

The CB radios Shawn had installed in all the vehicles worked well, enabling us to communicate with the castle until the range got too great. Their range, though, was much greater than the handheld walkie talkies we had and for local work, they would be of great use.

"The farm should be up the track coming up on the right," Louise eventually broadcast through the radio from her usual position beside Shawn in the cab of the tractor as we were driving along another narrow lane. Two minutes later, Shawn slowed down and cautiously turned the tractor onto an unmade road that led across some fields. With everyone on high alert, the small convoy followed, the vehicles rocking over the occasional pothole until from my position in the trailer, the farmhouse came into view.

The buildings looked different from the ground, but I knew it was a large place and from what I'd seen when flying overhead, it had been surrounded by a perimeter wall and the occupants looked to have barricaded all the entrances.

The armoured car pulled off the track and drew level with the tractor. Steve commanded us to stop a few hundred yards from the barricaded gate. Raising a pair of binoculars to my eyes, I could see some heads peering over the top of the wall looking back at us. One of the people I could see was holding a rifle.

"They look nervous," I spoke out loud. "But then again, I suppose that's to be expected." I called across to Steve. "Use the loud hailer to tell them it's us."

Steve gave me the thumbs up. The speaker on the armoured car screeched as he turned it on and his amplified voice boomed across the countryside.

"Hello. You have nothing to fear. We're the ones who flew over you a few days ago and we're visiting, like we promised. We've brought food and other supplies for you, so could you open the gate and let us in, please?"

"Gates opening," I called as I stared through the binoculars and saw two men, both with guns now slung over their shoulders, pushing the gates to the main farm open. Starting our engines, we slowly pulled forward.

***

The gates, I noticed as we drove through, had been heavily reinforced with wood and steel sheets. I nodded to myself with approval as I looked around the rest of the large yard, which from ground level seemed larger than I remembered from the air. It all looked secure. The height of the wall surrounding it had been raised using more sheeting and all the other entrance gates looked to be as reinforced as the one we'd driven through.

"These people seem to have got their shit together," I said with an air of approval to Eddy, standing beside me. "It looks as if they've done a good job here."

"They sure have," he replied as he went to open the door on the trailer so we could deploy the ramp to walk down to meet them.

Four men, three women and three children aging from about five to mid-teens were standing together, gathered by the front door to the farmhouse, looking apprehensively at us as we climbed down. When Ian shuffled down wearing his full armour, I smiled as they all let out an audible gasp of shock. Ian, Jamie and Geoff had won the coin toss as to which knights would accompany us. For the safety of those back home at the castle, we wanted to leave a few of them behind just in case they were needed. They all wanted to go and so to save a long discussion about it, we settled it on the toss of a coin.

Steve and I got out of the front of the armoured car, and we walked up to them, smiling as I extended my hand, saying, "Yes, they do look at bit frightening, don't they?" As I waved at the gathering knights, I added, "Trust me, under that armour they're all the biggest softies you'll meet and as daft as you like. I'm Tom, by the way," I said, shaking the hand of the oldest man there, assuming he would most likely be their leader. "Pleased to meet you."

The man, who looked to be in his sixties, shook my hand in return. His hands were coarse, probably from a lifetime of working the land. "Stuart. Stuart Brough," he replied simply. He then shook Steve's hand, eying his uniform as he did so. "Are you from the military?" he asked. His tone was not angry or curt but inquisitive.

Steve saluted as he replied, "Captain Steve Hammond. Yes, I am from the Army and my men and I are currently tasked to help protect these civilians," he said, indicating to us.

This time, the man's tone betrayed a touch of anger, "Well, where the hell have you been? My family and I have been trapped here since this began and we haven't seen anyone at all, let alone anyone in authority, until those men approached us yesterday."

Concerned, I blurted out before Steve could respond, "What men?"

This time, his face betrayed worry. "Just after sunrise yesterday, about twenty men approached us. All of them were armed. We didn't offer to let them in, and they didn't ask. We told them we had no food to spare as we were running out ourselves and they eventually left. There was something about them, though, which worried me. They were friendly enough, but they were asking too many questions about how many of us there were and other things. It was a bit odd, that's all. They wouldn't tell us where they'd come from or where they were heading to, just that they were in the area. At first, we thought it might have been you, because as I've just said, we haven't seen anyone since this began and with you flying over us a few days ago and then them turning up, the coincidence made it an easy assumption."

"I can assure you they were nothing to do with us," Steve replied, his voice calm and full of reassurance. "And as for the lack of help, I can only apologise on behalf of the Government, but as it stands," he then indicated to the other uniformed men behind him, "we are the only known combat effective force left on the mainland UK."

He left the statement to hang in the air as Stuart processed what he'd said. He staggered slightly with shock when he comprehended it fully.

"What? Just you? There must be more of you. You're the bloody British army, for God's sake. We knew things were bad from what we've seen, but we've been hanging on to the hope that help would arrive from the government at some point. It just has to." His face then filled with despair and fear as he continued. "Is it as bad as that?"

Soberly I replied, "Yes, it is. Now, shall we go inside so we can talk properly?"

The Broughs had farmed the land for generations. Fate had led the entire family to be there the day the outbreak occurred as they had gathered to celebrate Stuart's birthday. All three of their children, two of them married with partners there, along with three grandchildren, had gathered for what they expected to be a weekend of celebrations. Shocked, they'd watched the news story unfold on the television and listened to the radio, any ideas of having a celebration forgotten.

Abiding by the instructions on the government broadcast, they'd stayed together, continually monitoring all forms of media for updates and despaired when one by one, they went off air. They only left the farm to tend to the dairy herd that was grazing in their surrounding fields. Eventually and desperate to know what was going on, and with no other way of finding out, Stuart and his sons decided to go and check out the area around them. The trip had almost ended in disaster when they'd become surrounded by zombies in the nearest village. When Stuart recognised some of the zombies, the truth hit home and to save their lives, they were forced to drive over and through his former friends and acquaintances. Driving straight back to the farm, they began fortifying their home. Their grandchildren proved useful as they had more zombie experience from watching movies and television shows and told them what needed to be done.

For their safety, since they didn't know if they would be attacked, the cows were brought into their sheds and had been there ever since. Over the weeks, though, despondency had begun to settle over them all as their isolation weighed heavily on them and they tried to stretch out their dwindling food supplies.

Stuart had a tear in his eye when he explained they'd begun to consider the need to slaughter some of his beloved herd in order to feed themselves. It was only when they'd spotted our plane flying overhead and they'd read our messages that they realised they were not alone, and the cows had a reprieve. They decided to delay the decision until we showed up as we had promised we would.

"Did the food survive the drop?" I inquired.

His wife, Helen, replied with a smirk, "Most of it did, yes. Thank you so much, it really lifted our spirits just when we needed it. We've been so excited waiting for you to arrive. I could tell from your note that you're good people and now we've met, you've just confirmed it for me."

They were desperate to hear our story and so much had happened, it took quite some time to tell it, with different people adding their tales at relevant parts. They all knew Warwick Castle and marvelled at the scrapes we'd got into on our journeys there to make it a secure sanctuary. When Steve told them the news from the Royal Navy and the ongoing operation to make the Scilly Isles a base of operations, you could see their spirits lifting even more. They were not alone anymore and that gave them such a psychological boost. Knowing that others were not only surviving, as they were doing, but proactively working to help others, got the better of some of them. Emotion overcame them and tears of joy and relief flowed from eyes all around us.

Before any more discussions took place, Charles insisted on saying a few words. Not a prayer, but an acknowledgment of the struggles everyone had gone through and thanks for us uniting and our group being able to offer help to others.

The knowledge that a group of armed men were in the area worried us greatly. It didn't take much imagination to believe they'd be up to no good, because otherwise, they would have acted differently when they approached the Broughs. Our concern naturally turned to their security, so we asked them to first give us a tour of the property to see if we could suggest any improvements that could be made.

As we walked around outside, we could tell that with what they'd done by raising their walls and reinforcing the gates, the place was reasonably secure against zombies. It might not stand up to a vast horde of them but as yet, most likely due to their remote location, not one had even been seen in the area.

They'd always kept a lookout posted during the day by using ladders placed against the walls to see over them. We suggested a few improvements, such as the need to post a twenty-four hour watch now; to build platforms to use as firing steps and to improve the fences and walls in the surrounding fields to keep any zombies that might be in the area from getting close in the first place. It was clear, though, that the property needed better defences against human attack, especially after the recent visit. These details we handed over to the military contingent amongst us and with their permission, Steve commanded the sergeants to start planning and constructing what they could with whatever materials they could find.

As the work began, we got on with the main purpose of our visit. Did they want to come back to the castle with us now or in the future, or would they prefer to stay where they were? We told them that if they chose to stay, we would be able to supply them with enough food and other essentials and be able to offer what help we could with improving their defences. Stuart did have two shotguns and a rifle which he used to control the vermin on his land and was very happy when we told him he could help himself from the quantity of both rifles and shotguns we'd brought with us. Their guns had been easily accessible before, but they hadn't felt the need to keep them close to them until the visit by the group the day before.

The family was torn by the choices we gave them. Not having to worry about food would ease the burden on them enormously, but as their numbers were not great, would they be vulnerable to attack by both the dead and the living? We couldn't choose for them and sat quietly as the family debated what they wanted to do. Listening to them, it was clear they were torn between the two options.

Even though I was concerned for their safety, I liked the idea of another secure location being established and it was obvious that it could provide us with a good tactical advantage. We could extend our area of operations by using the farm to enable us to reach further afield and have a safe sanctuary to use, if need be. As their discussion continued, I decided to get Steve's attention and indicated I wanted a word with him.

We both walked outside. "What's up?" he asked. "By the look on your face you have a plan."

"Well, not a plan exactly," I responded. "Just an idea I wanted to run past you first before it goes any further." I paused to get the idea straight in my own head before continuing. "With the numbers they have here, they *are* vulnerable, especially now we know about the other group. My question is, could this place be fortified to act as an outpost?"

Steve looked at me and then at his men, who were working in the yard building defensible bunkers from hay bales and other materials. He was silent for a few minutes before he spoke.

"Anything can be made defensible if we have the tools and equipment, I suppose. It's manpower they lack. Even if the older child can use a gun, they'll still only have eight shooters and it's a big perimeter to defend. They could be in trouble if a horde finds them and we don't know exactly how many are in this group from yesterday. It doesn't take a military genius to work out they could easily be overrun."

"I thought so," I replied quietly. "I think we should recommend they come back to the castle with us. Unless there are more of them, their safety here can't be guaranteed. Unless, that is…" I stopped and looked at Steve.

"Unless what?" he filled in the silence.

I spoke slowly, unsure as to whether it was a good idea or not.

"Unless we station a few of your boys here, that is." Silence.

I stammered a reply to fill the silence. "We are more than capable of defending the castle with a few less. There are dozens of us who can fire guns. Here their defences are no way near as strong and they have far fewer numbers. If we balanced that out, do you think it would work?"

Eventually, his furrowed brows lifted, and he smiled at me. "That, Tom, is not a bad idea. Okay, then, they'll need some uparmoured vehicles and more of us to help bolster the defences until I'll be happy to station them here. If we start regular runs between both places, we can swap shifts when necessary…"

I held up my hand to stop him as I could tell he was getting into full flow. "Whoa there. It was only an idea I wanted to check was feasible first. It's not our home, so don't you think we need to see if they've made a decision yet?"

"Yes, of course," he replied, his voice now full of excitement at the prospect of another mission. "But I think it would work. Let's go in and talk to them."

CHAPTER TWENTY-FIVE

Inside the farm no decision had yet been reached about what the best course of action was for the family to take. Steve therefore asked for quiet so he could put forward a proposition.

"I understand that it's a difficult decision, but Tom has had an idea and I want to run it past you first." He waited until he had everyone's attention before he continued. "Now this is just an idea for now and nothing more. How about if I station a few of my men here to bolster your defences? I know we've only just met, but I hope you believe me when I say you can trust us, and that your ongoing safety is my primary concern."

"That's a generous offer," Stuart said cautiously. "Why would you offer that as well as everything else you've said you'll give us. As you say, you don't know us at all."

Charles spoke up, "You see, it's simple. It's not really ours to give. We already have more than enough to feed and equip ourselves for a long time and still we keep gathering more. Not because we are greedy, but because we have the skills and experience to do so in the full knowledge that others in the future may need what we've gathered. You're the first we've found and that lifted our hearts more than you could ever know. All our efforts haven't been in vain and at last, we can reach out and offer the hand of friendship."

He waved towards Steve, Eddy and Woody. "As for the idea of men being stationed here, I have known the two sergeants and the Captain for some time now and yes, they may swear at you when they catch you holding a gun wrong…"

Woody interrupted him with a snort of laughter.

"But you don't do it anymore, do you, Vicar?" he asked.

"Well, actually no I don't, so thank you, Sergeant, for your recent lack of profanities and the excellent training you've given me. But as I was saying, they are all as good a set of people as I have ever met. Most of us didn't know one another before all this began and now, we've formed a community I am proud to be part of. If any of the soldiers are stationed here, I can vouch for their character with no hesitation."

When he'd finished I noticed Stuart cast a glance towards his wife, who nodded in return. He then looked at the rest of his family, who were gathered around the table. "Does anyone have any questions?" he asked them all.

His son spoke up, "Dad, I know how much this place means to you; to all of us, in fact. It's been our home as well, you and mom raised us here and I know you've both said the only way you'll leave the place is in a coffin. But will we be safe here, even with the extra manpower?"

Stuart looked at me and Steve for an answer.

"Yes," I began, "I believe with a little time, we can make this place a small version of a castle. Within our group we have the skills and ingenuity to do most things. What you've achieved so far is impressive, we can just help you improve it. This farm could become an important link in the chain when, hopefully, we start to try and claim our country back. I imagine we'll need staging posts to start missions from and places to shelter and rest. I warn you, though; this place might get very busy at times."

His son nodded to me in thanks. "In that case, Dad. I think we should give it a go. If there aren't many of us left alive in this world, don't we owe it to everyone remaining to do what we can?" Then he laughed at himself. "Just look at me talking. A few days ago, we were talking about slaughtering Dad's cows so we could stay alive and now we're looking months and maybe years ahead. And his cows are safe! I can't believe it."

Stuart stood up and looked at his family. "Are we all in agreement?" All his family nodded in reply. He turned to us. "The answer is yes. We will stay here and accept your generous offer."

There was a general cheering and clapping from everyone in the room and the two groups merged and shook hands, smiles on the faces of us all. Steve sought out Stuart, saying, "Do you want to come and meet my men? I'll ask for volunteers and knowing them, there will be no shortage of those."

When he replied, "Of course. I'll be glad to," they walked outside and Steve called out to Sergeant Gallon to call his men together.

The sergeant was a stickler for discipline and a zombie apocalypse was not going to stop him fulfilling his duties as he chivvied the men into formation, his strong Geordie accent and standard sergeant phrases making Stuart chuckle.

"Ah, that takes me back."

"Have you served?" Steve asked.

"Yes," he replied, his gaze now looking to the distance as memories came back. "Did a few years in my younger days until I decided to take over the farm when my father was ill. Northern

Ireland mainly, but I did sneak in the Falklands before I decided to get back to civvy street."

Steve looked at the man with new respect. If he'd served in Northern Island at the peak of the troubles and took part in the recapture of the Falkland Islands, he was a tough individual, probably with plenty of valuable experience. He could sense from him, though, that he would probably not get much more from the man as many did not like to talk about their time in service. His comments marked him out as a Marine and he made a note to tell both Woody and Eddy about it. As fellow Marines, they would both enjoy meeting a former member of their elite band of brothers.

Steve shook his head with respect. "Not that I expect any re-sistance from them, but if they know you're one of us, so to speak, I'll expect even less now. Do you mind if I tell them you served?"

Stuart thought for a moment. Steve could imagine memories of his time in uniform flashing across his mind before, with a sigh, he responded.

"No, I don't mind. I just don't think about it much myself, really."

The men were now lined up before him, standing to attention with the sergeant eyeing them severely.

"At ease, men," he began, waiting a few seconds for them to change position before continuing. "Mr Brough has generously allowed us to begin establishing his farm as an outpost. A place that can offer sanctuary for patrols and enable us to eventually extend our area of influence. Mr Brough, as it happens, is one of us. He is a former Marine with active service experience, so he can probably teach us youngsters a thing or two." He smiled at them as he saw them all turn their eyes towards Stuart, who returned their gaze with a firm nod.

"Yes, chaps," Steve continued, "I know that means more hard work for all of us and for that I apologise." He waited for the polite chuckles and mock groans of the men to subside. "But as you know, we are it at the moment. I have no one else to call upon, so the burden once again falls on us few. To that end, I would like volunteers to come forward to act as the first garrison and to help to improve the security of this location. The details haven't been sorted yet and all I can promise you is more hard work with no real rewards, apart from the knowledge we're doing our utmost and continuing to honour the memories of the loved ones we've all lost."

Sergeant Gallon waited to be sure he had finished speaking before issuing his next command. "All volunteers, one step forward."

"Thank you, men," Steve replied after taking a few moments to control his emotions when every one of the men stepped forward as one. "We won't need all of you but once the details are sorted you will all get an opportunity to serve here." He took a moment to study the work that had already been started to help improve the defences of the farm. "You've worked hard in the short time we've been here. Please come inside for a well-earned mug of tea and a break while we plan the next step. Come and meet the rest of the family properly."

Following a short break, we formed a human chain and unloaded the supplies and other equipment we'd brought with us. The Broughs were delighted with the large pile of food once it was stacked in the boot room next to the kitchen, and we had to keep deflecting their continued offers of thanks. Stuart was also impressed with the firearms we unloaded. He picked up and studied one of the SA80 assault rifles.

I could tell he was proficient in handling them just by watching him. "It's a little different to the trusty old SLR I used," he said as he raised it and looked down the sights. "But I'll soon get used to it, I suppose."

We had brought a selection of shotguns, hunting rifles and assault weapons with us, along with plenty of ammunition for them all.

Eddy, who was carrying another case of shotgun cartridges into the house, heard him and said, "Ah, you can't beat a good old SLR, but I think you'll like it. They were a bit shit at first, but after several modifications, they got it right. When we get time later, I'll run through the cleaning and clearing drill with you if, you like?

Stuart put the weapon down and replied, "Yes, please. That would be useful. Can you show my children as well? They've been handling firearms since they were young. They were always out controlling vermin or rough shooting when they lived here, and all three are good shots." A worried look passed over his face. "It's a little different when shooting at a person, though, but they'll adjust, I'm sure."

Eddy stood and faced him. "Well, if they're like the rest of the civilians we have with us, they'll pick it up pretty damn quick when they need to." He shook his head in mock disbelief. "If I tell you the things I've seen our group of previously untrained civilians do, I think you'd have trouble believing me." He gestured to Jamie, who was helping move the boxes of supplies, trying to stack them as neatly as possible. He was still wearing his chainmail. "Wait until you see the knights in action. It's fascinating and bloody scary to see how well their tactics work. They hardly need us when they get started."

Stuart laughed in response. "I can imagine. When they first stepped off the trailer, I didn't know whether to laugh or shit myself."

***

As the day progressed and time wore on, real progress was made, shoring up their defences. A plan was also forming on the best way to improve them further. Stuart and I took Shawn, Steve, Eddy and Woody and walked the entire perimeter, armed with notebooks and measuring tapes to coalesce all the ideas we'd formed individually during our short time there.

The defences had to perform two functions; to protect the property against not only the undead, but potentially the living as well. The dead presented an easier problem to solve. You just needed high and strong enough walls to stop any getting inside. The initial defences Stuart and his family had constructed were, as we knew, sufficient, but with the experience and self-taught expertise we'd amassed in the short lifespan of the apocalypse, we knew we could improve them greatly. In fact, the work we'd completed since we arrived had already done much to better the situation.

Stuart had a backhoe loader on the farm which he used for cleaning out the cow sheds and other jobs. The moat that remained in parts around the walls of the castle provided an additional barrier that needed to be negotiated before the walls were reached, so we looked at the feasibility of digging a ditch around their entire perimeter. The excavated earth could also be used to build an earthen rampart that would provide another layer of defence.

A flaw in this plan would be that the berm could provide cover for any attacking forces who could use it to hide behind while launching their assault. As we toured the perimeter, we discussed the merits and pitfalls of the proposal and eventually decided it was worth doing. It was a big project but had the benefit that it wasn't labour intensive, as only one person was needed to operate the machine. We had other projects we'd choose to concentrate on initially; to reinforce the farmhouse so it could provide a well-protected fallback position if need be; further improvements to the firing steps that had already been started, and constructing some towers that would greatly improve their surveillance capabilities.

Stuart showed us what materials he had stored or lying about that we could use, and we drew up lists of what extras we needed. We still had a good quantity of materials that had yet to be utilised at the castle, and we worked out that with what we already had, we probably didn't need to go 'shopping' just yet.

As it was clear there was a lot to go at, after we'd asked and got welcome permission from the Broughs, we decided it would be best if we continued working throughout the day and stayed the night at the farm. If some of us returned to the castle in the morning, we would load up the supplies we needed to both work on their defences and for the garrison we were stationing there to use. The farmhouse had spare bedrooms which could easily accommodate extra personnel, but more occupants would obviously need more resources. A lot had already been given to them, but now that we'd met, we had a better idea of what they needed; more lists were drawn up.

Shawn and Stuart began marking out the moat, using posts hammered into the ground and before long, the sound of the loader's diesel engine filled the air as Stuart began work on it.

Many hours later in the gathering darkness, Steve called for us all to come into the farm for some much-needed food and a well-learned rest. After the meal, the guard rota for the coming night was organised by Steve. Those on the first shift went to their posts while the rest of us settled down to try and get some sleep, conscious of the early start we'd agreed for the morning to make the most of our time there.

I chose a comfortable looking armchair and before long, despite the quiet conversations that still flowed around the room from others who weren't as tired as me, I found my eyes drooping and I fell asleep.

***

I woke with a jolt as a loud repeated shout of, 'stand to!' came from outside, interspersed with flurries of shots. Initially confused, it took me a few moments to work out where I was. A whooshing sound and a flare of light through the window brought me fully awake. Eddy then screaming at the stop of his voice, "we're under attack, everyone to the defences," made me jump up and search for my weapon in the darkness of the room. Another flare of light from outside lit the room, helping me find my weapon, and grabbing it, I rushed outside along with everyone else.

Fires were burning fiercely in a few places. I looked up as an orb of flame arced over the walls and flared into a ball of yellow fire when it hit the ground.

Petrol bombs, my mind registered, processed, and then screamed back at me. "We're being attacked with petrol bombs!"

Confusion reigned in the courtyard as everyone seemed to be shouting at once. Eddy's booming voice galvanised us all into action.

"Everyone to the south wall. Open fire."

I ran to the nearest platform we had built against the south wall and scrambled up it. "What the fuck is going on?" I shouted at the shape beside me in the darkness as I aimed my rifle over the walls and searched for a target.

Steve's voice shouted back from my side. He was firing his weapon into the darkness. "Fuck knows. Some bastards are throwing petrol bombs by the look of it. It must be those from yesterday. Shit," he screamed in frustration "I can't see anything; we need some light up here."

"On it," I shouted in reply and, turning, I jumped from the platform and ran to the trailer. The flickering glow of the fires lit the area enough for me to find the bag I knew held some torches we kept in there. Grabbing it, I sprinted down its ramp. I was heading back to Steve when another burst of flame, this time on the walls, followed by screams of agony, made me stop in horror. A petrol bomb had exploded against the walls, covering two of our people with its dreadful contents. Both fell from the platform they were on and were writhing on the ground, their clothes and the ground around them burning fiercely. Inhuman sounding screeches of pain cut through the air. Dropping the bag, I ran towards them, pulling off my jacket which I threw over the nearest one to me in an attempt to smother the flames. I could sense others joining me as we desperately battled the flames, but they were soaked in the petrol which no matter how hard I tried, kept reigniting. Their continuous screams of utmost agony pierced my soul as I desperately fought to save their lives. Intense pain flared through my own hands as the flames scorched them, but I ignored it and furiously kept trying to beat out the flames. Over my own screams of panic, pain and fear, I could still hear guns firing relentlessly as those still on the walls fired their weapons at our unknown assailants.

A torrent of water came my way, unbalancing me and knocking me aside. It was quickly followed by more, which extinguished the flames on both men completely. I scrambled back to the person I'd been attending. His face was burnt beyond recognition so I couldn't tell who it was. I knew it was one of the soldiers, by the uniform he'd been wearing. He lay unmoving, his uniform still smouldering. Desperately, I tried to feel for a pulse but the charred shin on his neck and hands made it impossible for me to find one. I let out a howl of desperation. Looking over to the other body, from what I could make out from the uniform it had to be another soldier. He was writhing weakly on the ground and in the light cast by the fires still burning, I could see Woody and Louise feverishly tending to him.

More firing from the walls cut through the fog that had filled my mind. We were still under attack!

With a shout of, "Look after him," to the others I could see around me, I grabbed my rifle, retrieved the bag of torches and ran back to the walls. Steve was still firing his weapon outwards into the darkness and shouting commands to the rest of the defenders. When he saw the bag I had, he reached into it, pulling out a large flashlight which he immediately turned on. Its bright beam shot out across the fields beyond the walls. "There?" I shouted as in the beam's periphery I saw a figure. Steve adjusted his aim and the beam highlighted four people crouching about thirty meters from the walls who, as soon as the beam hit them, tried to scramble out of its glare. Screaming in blind rage, I raised my rifle, my finger automatically finding the rate of fire selector and I squeezed the trigger, sending a torrent of hot lead towards them. Even with my wildly aimed shooting it was hard to miss at that range and my bullets peppered the ground around them. Other defenders on the walls now adjusted their aim towards them when they saw them trapped in the beam of light and in seconds, countless bullets found their mark, killing them all as they tried to escape.

As soon as they were down, Steve moved the beam of light away from them and searched for more. The backs of distant figures running away were lit up and concentrated fire poured into every target until no more were found.

Steve kept scouring the area with the torch and after another five minutes when no more targets were found, ordered the cease-fire. He handed me the torch he'd been using and pulled another from the bag. "Stay here," he commanded. "I need to check the other walls."

Ten minutes later I heard him shout, "I think they've gone. Those on the walls, stay there and keep vigilant. Sergeants on me."

And then the pain in my hands hit me.

CHAPTER TWENTY-SIX

In dawn's early glow, I surveyed the damage. The blanket-covered corpses of the two soldiers lay in a corner of the yard. Their injuries had been too severe to give them any chance of surviving. The one I had tried to help had died as I was fighting to save him and the other a few hours later.

Everyone was too upset about our losses to pay much attention to the rest, but I'd noticed that the backhoe loader was burned out and still smoking and other fires had damaged some of the structures we'd built the day before.

As soon as it was light enough, Steve had led a patrol to investigate the surrounding area, primarily to check the bodies that lay in the field, but also to see if he could find any clues to the gang's whereabouts. Stuart's wife had treated my hands when they'd gone. They were both badly burned and in a normal world a visit to the hospital would definitely have been in order. As that was no longer possible, I had to settle for swallowing as many pain killers as I dared and to have my hands liberally coated with ointment and wrapped in bandages. I had to keep apologising for my language as she worked on me.

We gathered around expectantly as Steve, his sergeant and four other soldiers filed back in through the gate, carrying weapons gathered from the dead.

Anger as well as sadness played across Steve's face. "We know where they are," he stated simply as he sat on a bale of hay and ran his hands over his face. "One of the bastards was still alive and he told us before he died." He didn't tell us how he'd died, but we could guess. "Stuart?" he said as he picked him out from the crowd. "Can you show me on a map where this place is. It's some sort of hall or stately home or something."

When Stuart nodded, he stood up. "Get ready, men, we leave in ten minutes." His men cheered grimly at the news and reached for their weapons. Steve and his sergeant walked off with Stuart, presumably to get the location. As he passed me, he looked at my hands and his face softened. "Are you okay?" he asked.

I gingerly held my hands up, wincing as the movement caused a ripple of pain to spread through them. "I'll be fine," I said, trying to sound happier than I felt. "They'll heal." Looking him in the eyes, I could see grief as well as anger in them. "Is this a good idea, Steve?" I asked, "Don't we need to get our shit together before going up against them? Everyone's exhausted and not thinking straight."

He sighed; his drawn face lifted slightly as he smiled at me. "Normally yes, but if we delay, they'll move on. I don't think they knew we were here last night, they attacked expecting just minimal resistance from a group of civilians, not a barrage of automatic fire. If we give them chance to regroup, the chances are we'll never find them; they'll move on and we can't risk that. And as to exhausted, my men have just lost two more of their mates and are beyond angry. All they want to do now is get revenge on those bastards and if I don't do something now that we know where they might be, I think some of them will ignore any orders I give and take matters into their own hands and rush headlong at them. If I go, at least I can try and keep more of them from getting killed."

I thought for a moment. He was right, I was also full of anger at how they had died and quite probably, if I hadn't been injured and in so much pain, I, too, would have been baying for the attackers' blood. "Okay, mate, just be careful. There aren't many of us left, you know." He nodded and walked off.

I spotted Jamie, Ian, Geoff and Simon were also checking their weapons. Standing up, I walked over to them. "What are you doing?" I asked.

"We're going with them," Ian replied.

I shook my head slowly at them, "I wouldn't if I were you."

"Why not?" Ian asked defensively. "We knew them too."

"First of all," I replied carefully, "we need you here to help protect this place." I held my bandaged hands up. "I'm not up for much at the moment, am I? And secondly, I get the feeling Steve wants to keep this within his men. They've just lost some of their own and are out for revenge. He's going to have a hard enough time controlling them, let alone keeping you lot of maniacs alive."

Simon leant the sword he was sharpening against the wall. "So not a good idea is what you're saying?"

"Not this time," I replied.

Ian thought for a moment before nodding slowly. "Okay, agreed. Let's help the boys load up then, at least." As he passed me he held out his hand for me to shake. I instinctively took it and screamed out loud in pain as soon he gently touched it.

"Now that's what I call *not* a good idea," he laughed as he walked away, leaving me with tears of pain running down my cheeks as I tried to get my speech back to swear at him.

Within fifteen minutes, the armoured car raced out of the farmyard, clouds of black diesel fumes pouring from its exhaust as the driver coaxed every last inch of speed out of the vehicle.

Woody and Eddy closed the gates and dropped the locking bar into place, securing the compound. Charles spoke up. He indicated the two blanket-draped corpses. "I would like to bury those two brave men with dignity, if I may, Stuart?" he said looking at him. "Do you have a suitable place on your land you can suggest?"

Stuart looked painfully at the two corpses; tears formed in his eyes as he spoke. "Yes, Vicar," he said, pointing in a direction, "there's a beautiful copse of trees just over there. It's my favourite place on the farm and where I often go when I just want to sit and think. It has a beautiful view over the valley. It's where Helen and I…" he smiled at her as he took his wife's hand, "have stipulated in our will that we want to be buried. Those two brave men gave their lives to protect ours, so I'll be proud to lie by their side when my time comes."

"That sounds a beautiful place," Charles said. He turned to the sergeants. "Can you take me there so I can consecrate the land, please, and can you organise digging the graves?"

Woody replied soberly, "It would be my honour, Vicar." He thought for a moment. "We'll take my Land Rover for transport and protection if that's okay, but I suggest we wait until Steve and his men return before we do the service. Before we do anything, we do need to discuss what we should do today first. We need to get back to the castle and get more supplies for this place, but as last night proved, the ones left here might be vulnerable to another attack." He turned to Stuart and his family. "I've been thinking, would you be open to the idea of the women and children coming back with us until the work is complete? I can't guarantee their safety until then."

Stuart nodded in agreement, but his family initially looked shocked at the suggestion. He supported it because he could see it would be the safest option for them. They were resistant to it at first, but he slowly persuaded them and eventually, even though slightly reluctantly, they agreed to the idea. They just hadn't wanted to be separated.

I was excused work due to my injuries and took over guard duty as Woody drove off with Shawn, the Vicar and Stuart's two sons to begin work on the graves. Everyone else worked to tidy up the destruction caused in the night. The biggest loss was the backhoe loader, without which the ditch would be impossible to dig. Stuart claimed that he knew other farms in the area that had them, so they should be able to replace it easily enough.

The distant rattling of automatic fire made everyone stop and look around in fear. Deeper sounding bursts of fire intermingled with the continual noise. Eddy assured us that they were our guns firing and the deeper sound was the gun on the armoured car. After ten minutes or so, the noise slowed to the occasional burst.

"Looks like that's settled one way or another," Eddy informed us as he walked to Shawn's tractor to see if the CB radio was in range so he could get an update from Steve. A few minutes later he called out, "They've got them all, they reckon. They're doing a sweep of the area to double check and then they'll head back. Steve's reported no casualties on our side."

Most cheered with relief at the news and then redoubled their efforts to get ready for their return.

***

The burial was emotional for all of us who gathered around the two graves listening to Charles perform the service. Most of us had only known the two men for a short time, but their loss pained us as much as it did their brothers in arms, alongside whom they had served and fought.

Steve and Geoff, his sergeant, had both given a short speech remembering their time in service and the families they had both lost as the zombies spread throughout the country. Their speeches at times had us laughing as amusing stories were told and then wiping away tears as their sacrifice was remembered.

It was a sombre group that gathered in the yard of the farmhouse a short time later to make our final preparations to leave. The Broughs were all upset at their imminent parting, despite assurances from us that it wouldn't be for long as we would concentrate all our efforts on completing the works in as short a time as possible. Unfortunately, until we could find another ham radio, something we now needed to double our efforts to find, communication between the two sites would be restricted to messages passed by hand or mouth from the regular route we intended to start between us. We would experiment trying different routes to find the quickest way to reach each other. Once the optimal one was found that balanced speed with avoiding areas where zombies could mass and was cleared of any obstructions along the way, we knew the journey time would be reduced considerably.

Still though, the thought of being apart and out of touch was hard for them to bear. Steve left the armoured car and six of his men behind, and with Stuart and his two sons, Steve was confident they would have enough manpower to stay safe.

The latest threat, the gang that had attacked them, had been wiped out. The few survivors of the attack had, while they lived, been questioned and their story unfolded.

The gang had formed and grown as the apocalypse began. Initially, they'd just been a few frantic men who had banded together for mutual protection as they desperately tried to avoid the zombies. As their numbers and survival experience grew, though, their attitude changed. Continually on the move, trying to keep one step ahead of ever-present zombies, on the search for a safe place to shelter, they found some who refused to offer them help when they needed it most. Their initial attacks on others were more out of a sense of self-preservation than cruelty, but after encountering a few such groups, their mindset changed and the darker side of their personalities came to the fore. They had the strength in numbers, and nothing would stand in the path of their survival. Slowly moving through the countryside, they stopped asking for help from any they found and began attacking without provocation or compassion, always on the lookout for a suitable permanent base. Their survival took precedence over that of any others, no matter their situation.

Our arrival at the farm had gone unnoticed by them. After their discovery of them in the morning, they'd gone back to their temporary base and prepared to attack in their usual manner; in the middle of the night, when whoever they were attacking would normally be sleeping. They were not expecting the resistance they got. Shocked and reeling from their losses, they'd retreated to the house they'd taken over to lick their wounds. In cowardly manner, they were frantically getting ready to make good their escape from the area when Steve attacked.

Using their close quarter battle training, the soldiers had swept through the building room by room with maximum aggression and speed. The armoured car roamed outside, killing any who tried to escape through the many doors and windows of the house. The poorly trained, disorganised men inside had stood no chance against the onslaught. Given no quarter by the enraged troops, most had perished in the assault. Their story was gleaned from the few mortally wounded survivors before they succumbed to their injuries.

I did not feel sorry for them and the end they'd suffered. They could have used their group's strength and experience to help others, but instead took the other path, the more cruel, selfish and heartless one which ultimately led to their demise. They deserved everything they'd got as far as I was concerned.

The one positive thing I could take from their story was that they *had* found other survivors in their wanderings. Yes, they had attacked and killed those they discovered, but if *they* had found some, then there must be a far greater number still out there. All *we* needed to do was find them.

CHAPTER TWENTY-SEVEN

The relief of those at the castle when the CB radios were eventually within range was evident by the response we received. They'd known not to expect our return the same day, but the passage of time and the silence had only exacerbated their worries and fears about us.

Standing in the trailer, watching the countryside pass by as I scanned the area for any threats, I tried to keep my impatience in check, but I was desperate to see Becky and my children. This was the longest we'd been apart since the beginning of the apocalypse and I was missing them terribly. Everyone in the convoy was relieved that they'd had no problems at the castle to report. It had been a risk to separate as it left both groups weakened and at greater risk. A fact we knew only too well now, as two of us would not be returning. We hadn't broadcast the news of our loss because we thought it better to inform them face to face, knowing it would be taken badly by all. Both men had been popular and would be greatly missed. Their deaths were also a reminder to us all of the fragility of the lives we were now leading, no matter how well we all thought we were doing, no matter the quantity of our supplies, weapons and ammunition. Death or permanent disablement, as in the case of Marc, was an ever-present threat; only one wrong move or unfortunate event away.

I smiled grimly as the gates came into view and saw the knights standing at them, ready to push them open and let us inside our sanctuary. Driving through the grounds, I couldn't help but also smile at the Broughs, who were travelling in the trailer with me, gawking all around them and gasping with wonder at where they would be staying for the next few days. My mood, though, was sombre as we were about to tell people we'd lost two of our own.

As soon as the gates were closed and secured, I couldn't open the rear of the trailer fast enough so I could jump down and give my family the hugs and kisses I so desperately wanted to give them.

The claps and cheers and joyful barks of welcome sounded out as I ran into Becky's arms. These soon faded as they picked up on the mood as the others stepped from the trailer and Land Rover. Even the dogs stopped barking as they, too, sensed the solemn mood. Horace went to sit beside Ian and whined quietly for attention from him and Princess returned to Daisy's side.

Becky broke from my hug when she saw the tears in my eyes which she knew were not caused by happiness.

"What's the matter, darling?" she asked softly, her eyes darting around the rest of us, seeing how we all were carrying ourselves.

"We were attacked at the farm," I said quietly. "Danny and Rich were killed."

She recoiled in shock and looked around, trying to find them in the crowd as if to deny what I had just said. Holding her hands to her face, tears of her own filled her eyes.

"How…why?" was all she could say.

By now, I could see that the news was spreading by the growing reaction of the others around me. "Some bastards attacked the farm." I paused as I thought about the manner of their deaths, deciding it was best to spare Becky that knowledge for now. "They were killed defending the walls." I could see anger building in her face. "Don't worry, we beat off the attack and Steve and his men hunted them down and killed them *all.*" She nodded, waiting for me to continue. "They were a gang that had been roaming the country since this all began, not helping any they found, but killing and stealing from them instead. If we hadn't arrived when we did, the Broughs would have been overrun." Her brow creased as I mentioned the Broughs. "Of course," I responded at her confusion. "I haven't told you yet. The Broughs were the family at the farm." I indicated the group still standing by the trailer, looking at the displays of emotion all around them. "We've brought the wives and children back with us and some of Steve's men have stayed behind to help protect the place until we can improve their defences. We thought it would be for the best."

Becky looked at me as she wiped away her tears and a look of consternation rose on her face. "Well, this is some welcome they've been given," she said as she turned and walked over to them to introduce herself. Within minutes, others had caught up to the story and they, too, gathered around the new arrivals to welcome them to our community.

Maud once again took over by raising her fingers to her lips and emitting her customary shrill whistle, which quietened everyone immediately. "Now, it's getting late and nothing is being done by us all standing here talking. We have guests that need making welcome and I'm sure there are a lot of other things that need planning, if what I have been told is true. I suggest we reconvene in the Great Hall so we can begin." A small sob escaped as she said with eyes brimming with tears, "We also need to say farewell to Daniel and Richard."

As usual, she got it spot on. Twenty minutes later, mugs of tea had been made and distributed and apart from the children who were dispatched to guard duty, we all stood in a large group, chatting quietly about the events of the last few days and updating everyone on what they'd missed.

Charles asked for a moment's silence so we could remember those we'd lost, before he officially welcomed our new arrivals to our midst. Those of us who'd already begun planning what we would need to gather to take back to the farm split off and sat around the dining table and continued the discussion. Shawn, Jon and Chris produced the lists they had of the materials we had left over from the work we'd done on the castle. Steve joined us once he'd reported to the fleet.

As he sat down, I asked, "How's their mission going?"

He smiled tiredly as he responded, "It's all looking good. They have one final island to clear, but as it's one of the smaller ones, they're not envisaging many problems. Once that's cleared, they'll do one more sweep of all the islands just to be sure, and then they'll begin disembarking from the boats and ships on to St Mary initially and then they'll spread to the other islands. Hopefully, by the end of tomorrow they'll be in a position to do that." He looked at the notepad he was carrying. "They've asked a few questions which I hope we can answer."

"Fire away," I said.

"Firstly," he said, glancing at the pad and patting his pockets to find his pen, "do we know how much aviation fuel there is at the airfield?" He looked around the table until Shawn responded.

"The tank looked to be full, but I don't know how much it holds. As it'll be used to refuel all the planes there, I imagine a lot."

"Thanks," replied Steve as he wrote in his pad. "Secondly, how confident are we in our ability to gather more food?" He once more looked around the table before continuing. "Don't worry, I think I know the answer, but I didn't want to answer on everyone's behalf before I checked with you all. Their logistics guys are concerned about supplies. They have enough for an extended period but know that the Scillies won't be able to provide much to supplement what they have. Yes, there are fields that can be harvested and replanted and livestock already on the islands, not to mention fishing, but the supplies they have will be a finite resource that will eventually run out." He laughed. "The supply people must be bored because they're working on the feasibility of maintaining the islands in the long term as a permanent base."

The room went quiet for a period as we all thought about what he'd said. Eventually I broke the silence by saying, "I think the answer is we can get as much as they need but how will we get it to them?"

"Oh, let's not worry about that for now," replied Steve "It's the supply people asking the question. When they get the answer, they'll hand it over to us workers to come up with that solution, have no fear."

He stood up. "I'll go back with the answers. How are the plans coming along?"

Shawn beat us all to the response. "Good, I think. If we take the lorry as well as a tractor, we should be able to take everything we need. If anything else is required, there must be somewhere near the farm where we can get it, but what we have should make an excellent start."

"Great," he said. "The fleet are excited about the idea of using the farm as an outpost. They're interested to see how it works out for future planning when they start looking at the mainland." He turned and walked to the radio room.

Half an hour later, we'd drawn up the lists of materials and supplies we needed to take. This included not only construction materials but all the extra weapons and food that would need to be loaded. With not much more to organise, we cleared the table so we could all sit down and eat the food we could smell cooking.

CHAPTER TWENTY-EIGHT

At first light we began loading both the lorry and the trailer, checking items off the lists one by one as every available hand worked together. The Broughs had settled in well and despite their worries, helped us in the knowledge that the quicker we completed the work, the quicker they could get back to their loved ones.

The debate over the evening meal about who would go on the following day's mission had been hard to settle. We had to weigh up the need to protect the castle and the need to complete the work at the farm. The castle was secure against zombies, but now with the confirmed knowledge that there might be gangs roaming the country attacking those weaker than themselves, we needed to ensure we left enough people behind to defend the walls. We couldn't leave ourselves vulnerable for the sake of helping others.

With that in mind, only ten of us decided to join the convoy. With the ten already at the farm, twenty people working with the right tools and equipment should be able to complete the task in the timeframe we'd set; two days.

***

Trying to look as cheerful as possible, aware that the last time we'd left, two of us hadn't returned, I waved at my wife and children once more as we drove out through the gate.

Knowing the route better now, combined with the fact that it was clear of obstructions apart from the wandering zombies we barely slowed down to smash through, the journey to the farm took less than two hours and we arrived at midday. The good weather had broken as forecast, and those of us who were riding in the back of the trailer and lorry arrived wet and cold at the farm from the rain that fell. We'd all worn out sturdiest jackets and waterproof trousers, but the incessant rain had worked its way through zips and seams so by the time we arrived, most of us were soaked to the skin. The CB radios had warned Steve's men of our arrival and the warm mugs of tea they handed to us as soon as we stepped from the vehicles and trooped inside the farmhouse were very welcome.

All had thankfully been quiet at the farm. No one, either living or dead, had been seen and they'd got on with the necessary work, using what materials and tools they had. All the lower windows of the farm had been secured and firing positions created on various windows on the upper floors. Early that morning, one of Steve's men had used the armoured car to take Stuart to a neighbouring farm where he knew they had a similar digger to the one destroyed in the attack. The owners, who were also Stuart's friends, were still in residence. They'd all turned and they found them trapped in the house, their faces and hands pressing against the windows of the farmhouse when they were attracted by the noise of their arrival.

Stuart got to see the knights in action for the first time as they enticed them one by one from the house and killed them. Axes, maces and swords had quickly ending their misery. As well as taking the digger, they'd quickly emptied the house of any useful items they could find, including food and weapons.

On their return, Stuart had wasted no time in continuing the work on the ditch, while a planning meeting was held by the others to prioritise the jobs that needed to be done.

The work progressed well with so many hands to help and a determination to complete it in as short a time as possible. Although I was not much use and trying to accomplish any task with bandaged hands was a bit of a mission. The labour continued long into the night until exhaustion forced us to rest for a few hours, after which we dragged our tired bodies back outside into the rain and the growing light of dawn to continue.

By the end of the first full day, we all took a well-earned break to survey what we had achieved. The walls surrounding the entire place had been strengthened and raised. Towers had been built on each of the four corners. These gave a good view of the surrounding area and had been reinforced with steel and timber, which should make them resistant to small arms fire. Machine guns were mounted on two of the towers, and these would be able to lay down a withering amount of fire to sweep the fields surrounding the farm free of the undead, if they approached in large numbers. The work on the ditch was yet to be completed, but when it was, the plan was to line it with sharpened stakes to provide another layer of defence. The one vulnerable part of the walls would be the main gates; the other entrances had been blocked completely, so work had already started. Basing our plans on our experience at the castle, we built an extra angled set of gates in front of the main ones, which would direct any zombies into the deep ditches either side of it. We'd briefly discussed continuing the ditch in front of the gate and building a drawbridge over it but decided against it due to the difficulty of designing the winding gear needed to raise it. The rain we had endured had filled the ditch with water, so the place did begin to look as if it really was surrounded by a moat.

I looked at the much-diminished pile of materials we had unloaded. There was not much remaining, but then again, we seemed to have completed most of the work needed.

Shawn had concentrated his efforts on Stuart's tractor and silage trailer. It was the third one he'd performed his magic on, and his growing experience showed in how quickly he transformed them into a zombie-destroying mobile castle. Steve hoped that once the farm was secure, they would begin missions to reconnoitre the area in the search of survivors and supplies. The supplies would be stockpiled at the farm in one of its many outbuildings. What would happen to any survivors they found would depend on their circumstances. Stuart had already indicated he would be willing to allow more people to join them at the farm, saying it would be selfish of him not to permit it, following the kindness and generosity we'd shown to him. He did raise concerns that as they would be a much smaller group than us, whoever was allowed to join needed to be the 'right kind' of person; someone who would be able to get along with everyone and help them achieve their aims.

We assured him this would be the case, although his comments did make us realise how fortunate we had been so far, in that everyone we'd found had the right attitude and agreed with what our ultimate goal was. Had natural selection already weeded out most of the selfish and ungrateful or just unwilling from our society? Some bad apples would, of course, choose the other path, just like the gang we had just eliminated. We fervently hoped the former outnumbered the latter.

***

With shouts of 'see you soon' and other pleasantries, our much lighter vehicles left the following morning to return home. Steve was driving the armoured car with just one man operating the machine gun, while everyone else who was returning home lined the sides of the trailer and lorry, waving farewell to our newfound friends and the soldiers who were staying to garrison the place. As soon as we got back, Steve would return with the rest of the broughs and stay a day or two to settle in the men. His sergeant, Geoff Gallon, had volunteered to be the first to command the garrison, with the duty being rotated around woody and eddy as time passed.

I looked back at what we had achieved as we drove down the track. From the outside it looked formidable, a real outpost of hope in the midst of so much death and horror. I believed it would live up to expectations. Turning away, I settled down to watch the countryside passing by. Trying to protect my bandaged hands, I wedged myself into a corner of the trailer to avoid the need to hold on to the sides.

About halfway home, my eye was drawn to a flash of light. I turned my head and stared hard at where I thought it had come from. I could see the backs of houses in a village we were skirting around the edge of. I was about to dismiss it as the sun glinting of a window but then realised the day was too overcast for that, so I kept looking as we drove onwards.

"Stop!" I shouted when I spotted a light continually flashing from a window. Grabbing the binoculars and ignoring the pain, I raised them to my eyes and stared intently through them, searching for the source through the magnified vision. "There," I shouted again, pointing with my free hand. "Someone's flashing a torch at us though an upstairs window over there." By now, the vehicle had stopped and I was able to steady my aim. "I can see someone," I added excitedly. Ian picked up the walkie talkie to tell Shawn and Steve what I'd spotted.

We all knew without consultation that we would be going to help, so that was not debated. We just had to decide how to reach them.

The most direct route, straight to the house over the fields, was discounted because of the deep ditch that ran along the side of the road. Studying the map, we identified a lane coming up which led directly to the village, so without hesitation, all three vehicles, two lined with weapons held ready occupants, headed towards it. I could see it wasn't a large village, just a few houses surrounding a church, the spire of which could be seen rising above them all. It wouldn't be hard to imagine the layout from the many beautiful, small English villages I'd visited or driven through in the past. It probably contained one street lined with old houses, with a few new developments leading off from them. The church would be at its centre and if they were lucky, the local pub would have survived closure to still provide refreshment for all. It was how many unwelcome visitors we would find there that would be the only unknown quantity. And if whoever was signalling to us from an upstairs window was as desperate as the flashing light suggested, it didn't bode well.

When we entered the village it was easy to spot the building we needed to aim for. The front of the pub that faced the small village green was thronged with the undead, who began to peel away from crowding around its main door and started to head towards us when the noise of our arrival proved a more tempting target. The door to the pub was open and even though we couldn't see through its walls, I could imagine it was packed with 'customers' and the ones outside were pushing against them compressing them even further.

Raising his weapon, Eddy called out, "Thin them out, guys but watch your fire discipline. We don't know where they are in the building yet."

Individual cracks reverberated across the village as on single fire our bullets tore through the front ranks of zombies. Unable to hold my rifle, I watched the destruction the others were causing, grunting with satisfaction as the 5.56mm bullets punched holes though foreheads and faces, spraying the ones behind with their now very dead brains and virus infected blood. The vehicles we were in would protects us completely from what was stumbling towards us, and remorse or regret had long since been quashed in my emotions as I watched what was once another living person's life being ended. We had a job to do and by the way the corpses were beginning to pile up, forming a barrier the ones behind now struggled to climb over, we were getting good at it.

Not many words were exchanged between us all as the smoking brass bullet casings ejected from weapons rolled across the timber bed of the trailer. After every engagement, we diligently collected as many as we could find so they could be reloaded using the components and machines we had scavenged from the gun shops and then stored in the many boxes of bullets we had in the armoury. Bullets were a finite resource which needed to be husbanded carefully.

The outcome was as inevitable as it was gory and before long, the flow of bodies that had initially begun streaming out of the open main doors of the pub to join their zombie brethren had slowed to a trickle as the stragglers joined their now deceased comrades, hopefully in a more peaceful place.

"Let them clear the door before putting them down," called out Eddy. "Otherwise we'll have to climb over them to get inside, I imagine." We could all see this was a sensible idea, so there was a pause in firing as they waited for the remaining ones to get away from the entrance before they, too, were re-killed. Magazines were changed and new ones slapped home and the firing slowly decreased as the last few were killed. In the quiet that followed, I studied the pub. On a different day in a different life, it would have been an ideal refreshment stop on a sunny day. The piles of dead stacked in front of it now suited the gloomy, blustery, rain-threatening day it was now, though.

Movement in an upper window caught my attention. I could see three of four faces staring down at us. The pale, wide-eyed, terror-filled faces I could see seemed more scared than relieved. Which was understandable, as not for one minute did they imagine that the rescue they'd been so long hoping and praying for would turn up in armoured cars and Mad Max-style vehicles with everyone firing automatic weapons from them.

As the last crack of a rifle rolled away into silence when one late arriving, final zombie fell, I waved and smiled at the faces looking down on us in a vague attempt to reassure them we were a lot more friendly than we probably looked. There was more activity at the window and after a brief struggle with the latch, the window opened, and a bewildered looking man leaned from it. He opened and closed his mouth a few times, as if struggling to know what to say, before eventually settling for a brief, shaky sounding, "Hello?"

"Hi," I shouted back, trying to sound as cheerful as possible, "I'm glad we saw your signal. How long have you been stuck here?"

"Weeks," came the reply. "Since it began."

Putting his lack of chattiness down to shock, I carried on talking to try to get him to realise he was now safe, and we were not a threat.

"We were establishing a new base and were returning to our main one when we spotted you. We are, in a way, working under the authority of the surviving British military to begin establishing outposts, so we can create safe havens for survivors and safe places to gather and store supplies." The mention of the military worked, as I'd hoped it should. Any survivors would, I imagined, be expecting that the first help to arrive would be from the government itself and wouldn't present itself as we had in our ragtag collection of both military and converted farm vehicles. His face changed from shock to hope as I continued, "How many are you and are you okay for supplies?"

252

I didn't mention yet that we would be willing to let them come with us because I thought it might sound too pushy. They had to get used to the idea that they'd been saved first of all.

His response this time was more confident as he looked at us with renewed hope. "I'm the landlord of this place. I've got my wife and five villagers who managed to make it here. We're okay for supplies because the pub's storeroom is on the upper floors." He laughed. "And imagine how I used to moan about having to carry them all upstairs. I'm bloody glad we did now because otherwise we'd have starved long ago." He paused as he studied our vehicles with renewed interest. "Where have you come from? We heard you first and then caught glimpses of vehicles a few days ago and we've been desperately trying to signal to you every time you passed." He turned and looked back into the room and then turned and shrugged, a half smile on his face. "One of us even wanted to set fire to the building so you would spot us, but the sensible ones amongst us dissuaded him." I could hear a moan of mock protest from within the room and smiled back at him, saying,

"Yes, we have some who would come up with an equally dangerous idea. I caught sight of your light flashing out of the corner of my eye, so at least you didn't have to resort to that." I indicated to all of us and continued. "We've set ourselves up at Warwick Castle. There are over fifty of us now. Since we arrived, we've fortified the place and concentrated on gathering supplies." I spoke with genuine pride. "It really is an amazing place, where our children are as safe as they can possibly be, despite what's happening to the rest of the country; the world in fact. We're mainly civilians but as you can see, we're lucky to have the help of soldiers, too."

At my comment, Eddy spoke gruffly, his scarred face and general tough-looking demeanour contradicting the humour in his voice, "I'm a Marine, don't you include me with those soldier boys. We're the ones they call on when they're in trouble and can't tie their shoelaces or have run out of makeup."

Everyone, including the man in the window, laughed at his comment, which diffused any last traces of nerves or doubt he might have had about our good intentions.

I decided to ask the question, "Do you want to come with us? We've welcomed many into our group and we come from all walks of life, but what we've achieved together is incredible." I then added for effect, "We even have a vicar with us, but the true boss of our group is Maud, a lady we rescued from Bodmin Moor. She may be old and small but none of us dares get on the wrong side of her." I looked around conspiratorially and lowered my voice, "Don't tell her I called her old, though."

The man didn't even confer with those behind him as he replied, "Yes, please. We can't stay here any longer. We would have left weeks ago to find somewhere safer but," he pointed to the piles of bodies we'd created, "we couldn't get out."

"Great," I replied as everyone else in the vehicles let out a cheer of agreement. "Do you need a hand getting anything? We've got plenty of food, clothing and other supplies back home, but we have space for any personal possessions or anything else you might have that's useful. Give us a few minutes to clear a path to the door and we'll be ready for you."

"We can't get downstairs," replied the man. "We destroyed the staircase to stop them reaching us. We haven't got much in the way of food left but we can pack that up if you want. We do have a fair amount of booze left, though. There was a lot more, but we've had very little to do to amuse ourselves apart from card games, board games and the odd tipple or two."

My grin broadened at the thought of more booze being added to the already impressive stock we had. "Now you're talking. I don't think booze is one thing we can countenance running short of." I studied the building for a moment. "I tell you what. If we pull up to the front, we can raise a ladder and you can climb down. It'll be safer than scrambling over the corpses, especially since the sneaky bastards are sometimes hard to kill."

Ten minutes later, Shawn had used the plough to push the zombies into a grotesque jumble of death and the six occupants began climbing down into our trailer. After handshakes and warm welcomes were exchanged, a few of us climbed the ladder to help them pack up and load everything they wanted to take.

Once the last box of wine bottles was carried down the ladder, we stowed it and with a roar of engines, we drove off in the direction of home, chatting to the new arrivals, telling them the outline of our story with the promise of a full update when we were safely behind the walls of the castle.

EPILOGUE

The welcome we all received on our return was typical of our group. Everyone made a great effort to make our new arrivals feel as relaxed as possible, even the dogs, who seemed to be in competition to make themselves their favourites, just in case that meant more treats coming their way. The Broughs joined in with us all. They were returning with Steve, who wanted to refuel the truck and get back to the farm before night fell. The day was getting on due to our unexpected, but fruitful delay. Their brief time at the Castle had been spent usefully as they listened to and learnt from all our experiences, the mistakes we'd made and the successes we'd achieved. It was rewarding to see all that become shared knowledge, instead of just ours. The bonds that we formed would further bring our two groups together and more than one or two tears were shed by a few as last hugs and promises of 'see you soon' were shared. Finally, they climbed into the back of the armoured car to begin their return journey.

The sadness of our recent losses only marred slightly the celebration we held that night to welcome our arrivals, who were in awe initially at their new surroundings and marvelled at what we'd achieved when we gave them all a tour of the structure. Apart from Jake, the landlord of the pub and his wife Jenny, the rest only had the clothes they stood up in for possessions. They'd lived in deteriorating conditions at the pub as the water had stopped flowing, making washing and general hygiene increasingly difficult. They relished the chance to wash using hot water and put on the new clothes we got for them from our stores.

Following the meal, as Steve was absent, Willie took it upon himself to update the fleet as to our increase in population, while some of us put the children to bed and others retired to sit in the comfortable chairs of the Great Hall. The new arrivals had been told what was happening in the Scilly Isles and waited just as expectantly as the rest of us for Wille to finish and inform us of their progress.

Walking back into the room as we sat around the blazing fire in the Great Hall, he topped up his whisky and sat next to Maud, taking her hand into his as he did so, relishing the delay he was deliberately causing, evident from the cheeky grin on his face and the expectant looks on ours.

I broke the stand-off by blurting out, "For God's sake, man, stopping grinning like a Cheshire cat and just bloody tell us, will you?"

He theatrically took another sip of his drink before saying, "The mission is complete, and the Scilly Isles have been declared zombie free." He waited for the applause and cheers to die down before he continued, "Everyone is now disembarking from the ships and boats and accommodation is being allocated. They're having a few logistical difficulties in how to unload what's worthwhile from the container ships, because the port facilities on the island aren't capable of dealing with the larger vessels. But as the one thing they do have is enough people to help, they're confident a workable solution will be forthcoming soon enough."

Charles stood up and we remained quiet as he asked us all to give thanks for another landmark reached and the sacrifices that had been made to achieve it.

"Did they give any idea about what they plan to do next?" I inquired when he'd finished and returned to his chair.

Willie once again smiled and took another slow sip of his drink as he enjoyed delaying the next news. "All in good time, laddie," he said, winking at me and taking another slow sip until Maud this time spoke up. She slapped his leg and spoke sternly.

"Stop this behaviour, you silly man. You may think it's funny, but you are being rude and not amusing at all. If you don't tell us now, I will hide those whisky bottles you think you have hidden away from me. I know exactly where they are, and you will never find them if I move them."

Instantly contrite at being told off by his beloved Maud and the thought of his not-so-secret stash being impounded, to our amusement he went red with embarrassment and his eyes went wide with fear.

"Och, I'll tell," he blurted out quickly and put his glass down. "They're going to spend the next few days getting settled, but there's an aeroplane at the island's runway. It's a small passenger plane. "That has the range to reach us and as soon as they are able to, they're planning to visit us so we can have a council of war on what the next stage of the plan should be."

That was exciting news and we all started talking over each other at once and the general noise in the room grew, until Maud emitted her customary whistle, short this time and not as loud as usual,, which quietened us all down immediately.

"One at a time, you'll wake poor Sarah up if you carry on like this."

***

Four days later, we waited expectantly at Wellesbourne Airfield. The armoured car and Shawn's tractor were patrolling the perimeter on the lookout for any unwanted visitors, while Steve and I and a few others stood by the apron, staring in the direction we knew the plane should be approaching from.

"There it is," shouted Steve excitedly, his younger eyes picking out the small speck in the blue sky a few seconds before the rest of us did. Steve spoke via his radio to those patrolling the perimeter, before telling the soldier who was manning the radio in the tower to confirm to the arriving plane that all was clear.

I let out an inner sigh of relief when the propeller-powered passenger plane touched down smoothly and I waited impatiently for it to clear the runway and make its way along the taxi way to where we were standing by the tower. As the engine noise quietened down and the propellers slowly stopped turning, the door on the side of the plane opened. When the inbuilt steps had unfolded, a man wearing a splendid looking uniform walked down them and headed straight for us. Extending my hand to shake his, my smile broadened, and a great feeling of accomplishment and achievement came over me.

We were alone no longer; from a desperate beginning we had survived. From sleeping rough in the wilds of Bodmin Moor after barely escaping from St Agnes, our numbers had increased and our experience and skills in surviving the terrors of a zombie apocalypse had grown with each passing day. Never wavering as we set out to achieve the goal we'd set for ourselves that very first night sitting around a fire in the darkness, we'd reached the perfect sanctuary that was Warwick Castle. We hadn't rested then, but had still worked tirelessly, our numbers increasing as Willie and the soldiers joined us. With our growing confidence, we began searching for other survivors, locating them initially by using a plane from the airfield I was at now.

We now had another community in a secure location we had helped to establish, who were just as willing as we were to answer the call from the remnants of the armed forces who had survived the devastation to help their country.

We were now going to discuss the best way forward to begin to make the British Isles not a union of countries populated by the undead, but one where the living held sway.

Chris Harris is a UK-based author, well-known for his post-apocalyptic and zombie book series.

Find his website at www.chrisharrisauthor.co.uk

Facebook @chrisharrisauthor

UK Dark Book 1: The Blackout

By Chris Harris

"What would happen if……?"

Many people ask themselves the question, but how many actually do something about it?

Tom lives in Birmingham, England with his family. After asking himself the question and researching what could happen, he decided it wouldn't do any harm to be a little bit prepared. Just in case.

He discovers the world is going to be hit by a massive Coronal Mass Ejection from the sun, which will turn the whole planet dark.

He only has a few days to get ready.

Will they survive?

People want what they have, but is he prepared to kill to protect it?

The UK Dark series, out now!